Heidi

Lessons at Home and Abroad

Heidi

Lessons at Home and Abroad

Johanna Spyri

Translated by
Peter James Bowman

Illustrations by
Susan Hellard

ALMA CLASSICS

ALMA CLASSICS
an imprint of

ALMA BOOKS LTD
3 Castle Yard
Richmond
Surrey TW10 6TF
United Kingdom
www.almajunior.com

Heidi: Lessons at Home and Abroad first published in German in 1880
This edition first published by Alma Books Ltd in 2017

Translation © Peter James Bowman, 2017

Inside and cover illustrations © Susan Hellard, 2017

Extra Material © Alma Books Ltd

Printed in Great Britain by CPI Group (UK) Ltd, Croydon CR0 4YY

ISBN: 978-1-84749-665-2

Contents

Heidi

Lessons at Home and Abroad

Chapter 1

Going up to the Alp Uncle

FROM THE PICTURESQUE old village of Maienfeld there is a footpath that leads through green, wooded meadows to the foot of the grave, lofty peaks overlooking this side of the valley. Where the path begins its ascent, the rambler soon encounters the fragrance of short grass and strong mountain herbs wafting across from the pasture, for the way now leads steeply and directly to the alps.

On a sunny morning in June, a tall, sturdy-looking young woman of this mountainous region was climbing up the narrow path, holding by the hand a small child whose cheeks were so flushed that their glow lit up the deep brown of her suntanned skin. And no wonder, since despite the blazing June sun the child was wrapped up as if she needed protection against a severe frost. She looked barely five years old, but it was impossible to make out her natural form, as she was evidently wearing two if not three dresses, one on top of the other, and then a large red cotton scarf wound round and round, so that her little figure was quite shapeless above her heavy, hobnailed mountain shoes as she toiled hotly uphill.

The two travellers must have had an hour's climb from the valley by the time they reached the settlement halfway up the pastureland simply known as the "little village". Here people in almost every house called out to them, from windows and doors and from the roadside, for the young woman was in the place of her birth. But rather than stopping and standing still, she responded to the shouted greetings and questions in passing until she came to the last of the small, scattered houses at the end of the village. Here a voice called from a doorway: "Wait a second, Dete. If you're going higher I'll come with you."

Now Dete stood still, and immediately the child freed herself from her hand and sat on the ground.

"Are you tired, Heidi?" asked her companion.

"No, I'm hot," answered the child.

"We'll be there soon," said the other encouragingly. "Just keep going a bit longer and take big strides, and we'll be up in an hour."

At that moment a stout, kind-looking woman stepped out of the house and joined them. The two old acquaintances then walked on and launched into an animated conversation about various inhabitants of the village and nearby dwellings. Heidi, having got to her feet, followed behind.

"But where are you taking the child, Dete?" asked the other woman. "I'm guessing she's your sister's girl, the orphan."

"That's right," Dete replied. "I'm taking her up to the Alp Uncle. She's to live with him."

"What, live with the Alp Uncle? You must be out of your mind, Dete. How could you do such a thing? In any case, the old man will send you and your plan packing at once!"

"He can't. He's her grandfather and he has to help. I've kept the child till now, but you can take it from me, Barbel, I'm not giving up a post like the one I've been offered for her sake. It's time her grandfather did his bit."

"That would be fair enough if he was like other people," said the stout woman warmly, "but you know how he is. He'll have no idea what to do with a child, especially such a small one! She won't be able to stand it! By the way, where is it you're going?"

"Frankfurt, and a first-class household. The family were down at the baths last summer and I saw to their rooms, which were on my corridor. They wanted to take me back with them then, but I couldn't get away. And now they're here again and want to take me, and believe me I want to go."

"I don't envy the child," exclaimed Barbel, throwing up her hands in horror. "No one knows what makes the old man up there tick! He wants nothing to do with anyone, he doesn't set foot inside a church year in, year out, and when he comes down every twelve months or so with his big stick everyone takes fright and steers clear of him. With those bushy grey eyebrows and that terrible beard he looks like an old heathen or a Red Indian, so that you're glad if you don't bump into him."

"That doesn't change the fact that he's the child's grand-father and must take care of her," Dete said defiantly. "He won't do her any harm, and if he does, he'll have to answer for it, not me."

"All I want to know," Barbel said, probing, "is what the old man has on his conscience to give him such a wild expression and make him live like a hermit up on the pastureland, hardly ever showing his face. People say all sorts of things about him, but you must have some real information from your sister. Am I right?"

"Of course, but I'm not telling! If it came to his ears I'd be in a pretty pickle!"

Barbel had long wished to know how matters stood with the Alp Uncle, why he looked so cross with the world and lived all alone so high up, and why people talked about him evasively, as if they were afraid of making an enemy of him but didn't want him as a friend either. And Barbel also had no idea why the villagers called him Alp Uncle: he couldn't be a real uncle to all the inhabitants of the place. But as everyone called the old man by this name, using the local dialect word for "uncle", so she always did too.

Barbel was a recent arrival, having moved to the village as a bride. Prior to that she had lived down in Prättigau, and she was not yet familiar with all the past and present personalities and goings-on in the village and its environs. Her friend Dete, on the other hand, had been born in the village and had lived there with her mother until the latter's death a year before. Then she had moved to Ragaz, where she earned a good living as a chambermaid in the big hotel there. She had come all the way from Ragaz that very morning, getting a lift to Maienfeld for herself and the child on a hay wagon that a friend of hers was driving home. Barbel did not want to waste this opportunity of adding to her store of knowledge. She took Dete familiarly by the arm and said: "You're the person to say what's true and what's just idle talk. You must know the whole story. Tell me a bit about the old man. Has he always hated and frightened his fellow men so?"

"Whether he's always been like that I couldn't exactly say. I'm twenty-six years old, and he must be seventy, so you can't expect me to have known him when he was young. But if I could be certain my words wouldn't be doing the rounds of Prättigau afterwards, there's a lot I could tell you about him. My mother came from Domleschg just as he did."

"Pah, Dete, what do you mean?" Barbel retorted, a little offended. "Prättigau isn't such a terrible gossip mill, and as for me I can hold my tongue if need be. So do tell me – you won't regret it."

"All right then, but keep your word," Dete warned her.

Then she glanced round to make sure the child was not close enough to hear what she was going to say. But she was nowhere to be seen. She must have stopped following some way back, and they had been too engrossed in their conversation to notice. Dete came to a halt and looked all about her. Although the footpath twisted and turned it was visible almost as far down as the village, but there was no one on it.

"There she is," said Barbel, pointing to a spot some distance from the path. "Can you see her? She's climbing up that steep slope with Peter and his goats. I wonder why he's out with them so late today. It suits me, though, because if he looks after the child you'll be free to tell me your story."

"Looking after her won't cost Peter much effort," Dete remarked. "She's bright for a five-year-old. She keeps her eyes peeled and sees what's going on around her, I've noticed. And that will stand her in good stead one day, because the old man has got nothing now beyond his two goats and his cottage on the pastureland."

"Did he use to have more, then?" asked Barbel.

"Have more? Yes, he certainly did," Dete replied quickly. "He had one of the best farms in the Domleschg valley. He was a first son with just one brother – a quiet, sensible lad. But all he himself wanted was to act the fine gentleman and drive about the country and get in with a bad lot, people nobody knew. He drank and gambled away the whole property, and when it came to light his father and mother died of sorrow, one after the other, and his brother, who was likewise reduced to beggary, was so sick at heart that he went into the wide world, not a soul knows where. The Alp Uncle himself, with nothing left but his bad reputation, also disappeared. At first his whereabouts were a mystery, then it came out that he had gone to Naples as a soldier, and then no more was heard of him for twelve or fifteen years. One day he suddenly reappeared in Domleschg with an adolescent boy and wanted to find a home for him among his relatives. But every door was closed in his face, and no one wanted anything to do with him. He was so infuriated that he vowed never to set foot in Domleschg again, and then he came to the village and lived here with Tobias, the boy. The mother was a native of Graubünden that he had met most probably on his travels, and who had died not long after. He must still have had some money, because he found a place for Tobias to learn a trade, carpentry. He was a steady youth and well liked by all in the village. But no one trusted the old man, and people said he had deserted in Naples to get out of a scrape he was in, because he had killed a man – not in battle, you understand, but in a brawl. Our family did acknowledge him as a relation, though, since my mother's grandmother and his grandmother were sisters. That's why we called him Uncle, and as we're related to almost everyone in the village on our father's side they all called him Uncle too, and ever since he went to live up the mountainside he's been known simply as Alp Uncle."

"But what happened to Tobias?" Barbel asked eagerly.

"Hang on, I'm just getting to that. I can't say everything at once. Well, Tobias was apprenticed over in Mels, and when he'd finished there he came home to the village and married my sister Adelheid. They'd always been fond of each other, and they got on very well together as husband and wife. But it wasn't to last. Two years later, while Tobias was working on a house that was being built, a beam crashed down and killed him. And when her husband was brought home all disfigured, the horror and agony of it put Adelheid in a violent fever that she didn't recover from. She'd never been strong, and sometimes she had funny turns where you didn't know if she was awake or asleep. Just a few weeks after Tobias's death they buried her too. Far and wide people spoke of the couple's tragic fate, and they said – in whispers or out loud – that it was a punishment Uncle had drawn on himself for his godless life. Some said it to his face, and the pastor appealed to his conscience and told him he should now repent. But he grew more and more grim-faced and obstinate and wouldn't talk to a soul, and everyone kept out of his way. One day we learnt that he'd moved up to the pastureland and wouldn't be coming back, and since then he's lived there, at variance with God and his fellow men. Mother and I took in Adelheid's little girl. She was a year old at the time. And when Mother died last summer and I wanted to start earning a living in Ragaz, I took the child with me and boarded her out with old Ursel up in Pfäfers. I was able to stay in the resort during the winter; there was plenty of work as I'm a good needlewoman. And in early spring the family from Frankfurt came again, the people I'd served the previous year and who wanted to take me back with them. We're leaving the day after tomorrow, and it's a good position, I can tell you."

"And you're going to hand the child over to the old man? I don't know what you can be thinking of, Dete," said Barbel reproachfully.

"What do you mean?" Dete shot back. "I've done my bit for her, and what am I supposed to do with her now? I don't think I can take a child just turned five along to Frankfurt. But where is it you're going, Barbel? We're a fair way up the pasture already."

"I'm nearly there," replied Barbel. "I have to speak with Peter's mother; she does some weaving for me in winter. Farewell then, Dete, and good luck!"

Dete shook her friend's hand and then stood and watched as she walked over to the small dark-brown cottage situated in a sheltered hollow a few steps to the side of the path. The cottage was about halfway up the pasture, as measured from the village. It looked so ramshackle and dilapidated that its position in a small dip on the mountainside was fortunate, but even so it must have been dangerous to be inside when the föhn wind tore across the slopes with all its might, making everything rattle inside – the doors, the windows and the rotten beams. Had the cottage been high up on the pastureland on such days it would very soon have been swept into the valley below.

This was the home of Peter the Goatherd, an eleven-year-old boy who each morning went down to the village to fetch the goats and drive them to the upper reaches of the pasture, where they munched on the short, strong herbs. In the evening Peter scampered with the nimble creatures back to the village, and their owners collected them from the square on hearing him whistle sharply through his fingers. It was mainly small boys and girls who came, the goats being too gentle to inspire fear, and throughout the summer this was the only time of day when Peter saw children his own age; otherwise the goats were his sole companions. He lived with his mother and blind grandmother, but he was rarely with them, because he had to set out very early in the morning and returned from the village late after spending as much time as he could chatting with the other children. Indeed, he only had enough time at home to swallow his bread and milk in the morning and the same meal at night before putting his head down to sleep. His father – also called Peter the Goatherd because he had done the same job in his youth – had lost his life in an accident while felling trees a few years earlier. His mother's name was Brigitte, but she was universally known by association as the Goatherd's Mother, while the blind old woman was simply called Grandmother by young and old alike in the whole vicinity.

Dete waited a good ten minutes and looked out in all directions for the children and the goats, but in vain. Then she climbed a little higher to get a better view right down the mountainside, and from this spot she peered this way and that, her face and gestures betraying great impatience. Meanwhile the children approached along a lengthy byway, for Peter knew many places with all sorts of wholesome bushes and shrubs for his goats to nibble on, and to this end he made a variety of detours with his herd. At first the girl clambered laboriously after him, gasping with heat and discomfort under her heavy layers of clothing. She said nothing, but looked intently at Peter, who jumped effortlessly back and forth in his short trousers and bare feet, and then at the goats, whose light, slender legs carried them even more easily over bushes and rocks and up steep slopes.

All of a sudden she sat on the ground, rapidly removed her shoes and stockings, then stood up again, pulled away her thick red scarf and undid her dress. She whipped it off and started unfastening a second, for her Aunt Dete had simply put her Sunday dress over the everyday one to save time and the trouble of carrying it. The everyday dress also came off in an instant and the child stood in her light, short-sleeved petticoat, joyfully throwing her bare arms in the air. Then she made a neat little pile of her garments and began leaping and scrambling at Peter's side after the goats, moving as freely as any of them. Peter had paid no attention to what the girl was doing when she fell behind, and he grinned across his face when she came bounding after him in her new costume. He looked back, and the sight of the pile of clothes made his face crease up even more, till his mouth stretched almost from ear to ear. But he said nothing.

The unburdened girl, feeling much more at ease, started talking to Peter. He found his voice too and had all sorts of questions to answer: she wanted to know how many goats he had, where he was going with them and what he would do when they got there. Eventually the children arrived with the goats at the cottage, where Dete still stood.

The moment she spotted the group making their way towards her, she shrieked: "Heidi, what have you done? Just look at you! Where are your dresses and scarf? And the brand-new shoes I bought you for the mountain and the new stockings I made for you. Gone, all gone. What have you done, Heidi? Where is it all?"

Calmly the girl pointed down the mountainside and said, "There!" Her aunt followed the line of her finger and saw that there was indeed something on the ground, with a red dot – no doubt the scarf – on top.

"You little wretch!" she shouted in vexation. "What were you thinking of? What do you mean by taking it all off?"

"I don't need it," said the child, showing no remorse at what she had done.

"Oh, you cursed silly girl, are you out of your senses?" her aunt berated her plaintively. "Who's going to go back down and fetch the things? It's half an hour's walk! Peter, you go for me, and be quick about it. Don't just stand there gawping at me as if you were nailed to the spot."

"I'm late as it is," said Peter slowly, his hands in his pockets, not budging an inch from where he had been during her horrified outburst.

"You won't get far by standing still with your eyes staring out of your head," Aunt Dete exclaimed. "Come here, I've got something nice to give you. See this?" And she held out a new five-rappen piece that glittered before his eyes. Instantly he perked up and made off by the shortest route down the mountainside, and before long his giant strides brought him to the pile of clothes. He gathered them up and reappeared so fast that Dete could only praise him and hand over the coin straight away. Peter promptly thrust it deep in his pocket, his face beaming from side to side, for such riches rarely came his way.

"You can carry the things up to the Alp Uncle's house if you're going there too," Dete added, as she prepared to ascend the steep incline directly behind the cottage belonging to Peter's family. He gladly did as he was asked and followed on her heels, the bundle draped over his left arm and his right hand waving his goatherd's switch. Heidi and the goats skipped and jumped about gleefully beside him.

Three quarters of an hour later, the procession reached the top of the pastureland, where the Alp Uncle's cottage stood alone on a spur of the mountain, exposed to all winds but also to every ray of sunshine and with a clear view deep into the valley. Behind the cottage were three old fir trees with long, heavy, unlopped boughs. Beyond these the land rose up towards the grey, rocky cliffs, first over pretty expanses of grasses and wild herbs, then across rock-strewn scrub, and finally to the bare towering peaks.

Attached to the cottage and facing the valley was a bench the Alp Uncle had carpentered. Here he sat, a pipe in his mouth and his hands on his knees, and watched calmly as the children, the goats and then Dete, who had gradually been overtaken by the others, worked their way up towards him. Heidi arrived first, went straight to the old man and said, "Good afternoon, Grandfather!"

"Well, well, what's the meaning of this?" the old man asked in a gruff voice as he briefly shook her hand and fixed her from under his bushy eyebrows with a long, penetrating stare. Heidi held his gaze for some moments without blinking even once. With his long beard and the dense, grey eyebrows that grew together over his nose like some sort of thicket, her grandfather was a remarkable sight, and she had to have a good look at him. Meanwhile Dete walked up to them together with Peter, who came to a stop and waited to see what would happen next.

"Good day to you, Uncle," said Dete as she approached. "Today I'm bringing you the daughter of Tobias and Adelheid. You probably won't recognize her, as you haven't seen her since she was a year old."

"I see, and what am I supposed to do with her?" said the old man curtly. "And you there," he called over to Peter, "you can be off with your goats – you're late as it is. And take mine with you!"

Peter obeyed and disappeared at once, because the way the Alp Uncle looked at him made him feel uneasy.

"She'll have to stay with you, Uncle," replied Dete to his question. "I think I can say I've done my duty by her these last four years, and now it's your turn to do something."

"I see," said the old man, turning his flashing eyes on Dete. "And if she starts whimpering for you and making a fuss like children her age do, then what am I supposed to do?"

"That's your business," Dete retorted. "I don't think anyone told me how to look after her when she was left in my charge, just twelve months old, and me with enough to do already for myself and Mother. Now I need to go to my new employment, and you're the child's next of kin. If you can't take her in, make whatever arrangement you like. But it will be your responsibility if she goes to the bad, and I should think you have enough on your conscience as it is."

Dete's own conscience was troubled by the whole affair, and this had made her grow heated and say more than she had intended. At her last words, the Alp Uncle got to his feet and gave her a look that caused her to shrink back a few steps. Then he raised his arm and said in a commanding voice: "Get yourself back down to where you came from, and don't be in a hurry to show your face here again!"

She didn't wait to be told a second time. "Farewell to you – and to you, Heidi," she stammered, and then she hurried down the mountain to the village without stopping, the agitation in her breast driving her on like a steam engine. This time even more people called out to her as she passed through the village, curious to know where the child had got to. Dete was well known to them all, and they also knew who the child's parents were and what her previous history had been.

From every door and window came the cry: "Where is the child, Dete? Where have you left her?"

"Up with the Alp Uncle! With the Alp Uncle, I said!" she shouted more and more irritably.

Then she became really annoyed, because from all sides the women cried out: "How could you do such a thing?" and "Poor little mite!" and "To leave such a helpless little thing up there!" And then again and again: "Poor little mite!"

Dete rushed on and on as fast as she could, and was relieved when she could no longer hear their voices, for she felt uneasy herself at what she had done. Her mother had entrusted the child to her on her deathbed. However, she comforted herself with the thought that she could do more for her when she was earning good money, and she was very glad that her excellent new position would take her far away from all the people who were trying to interfere.

Chapter 2

At Grandfather's

ONCE DETE HAD GONE, the old man sat back down on the bench and blew out great puffs of smoke from his pipe. He stared at the ground in silence. Heidi looked contentedly about her and discovered the goat pen that had been built onto one side of the cottage. She peered in, but it was empty. Continuing her exploration, she came to the old firs behind the cottage. The wind blew so forcefully across the boughs that the treetops hissed and whistled. Heidi stood still and listened. When the noise died down a little, she went on with her circuit of the house and rejoined her grandfather. Finding him in the same posture as before, she planted herself in front of him with her hands behind her back and observed him.

Grandfather looked up. "What do you want to do now?" he asked, seeing the child still motionless before him.

"I want to see what you have inside, in the cottage," replied Heidi.

"Come on, then." And Grandfather stood up and led the way: "Pick up your bundle of clothes over there and bring them in."

"I don't need them any more," she said.

The old man turned round and looked searchingly at the child, whose black eyes shone in expectation of what she would find indoors. "She can't be stupid," he said in an undertone. "Why don't you need them any more?" he said aloud.

"I'd rather move about like the goats. They're so light-footed."

"So you can, but fetch the things," Grandfather ordered. "They can go in the cupboard."

Heidi did as she was told. The old man now opened the door, and Heidi stepped behind him into a fairly large room that filled the length and breadth of the cottage. The room contained a table and chair; in one corner was Grandfather's bed, and in another a big pot hung over the stove. On the far side was a large door in the wall that Grandfather opened to reveal a cupboard. In it hung his clothes, with a few shirts, socks and handkerchiefs on one shelf; some plates, cups and glasses on another; and on the top shelf a round loaf, smoked meat and cheese. The cupboard held all the Alp Uncle's possessions, everything he needed to subsist. As soon as he opened it, Heidi ran forward and thrust in her things as far as she could, right to the back behind Grandfather's clothing, so that they could not easily be retrieved. Then she looked around the room with close attention and asked, "Where am I going to sleep, Grandfather?"

"Wherever you like," he replied.

That suited Heidi perfectly. She rushed all over the room looking into every nook to find the best place to sleep. In the same corner as Grandfather's bed was a small ladder propped against the wall, and Heidi climbed up and went into the hayloft. There she found a pile of fresh, sweet-smelling hay and a round skylight with a view right down into the valley.

"This is where I'll sleep," Heidi called down. "It's lovely here, Grandfather! Come and see!"

"I know," came the voice from below.

"I'm just making the bed," the girl shouted as she bustled to and fro, "but please come up and bring me a sheet, because a bed needs a sheet before you can lie on it."

"Is that so?" said Grandfather, and presently he went to the cupboard and rummaged inside. From under his shirts he drew out a large cloth of coarse linen that could serve as a sheet, and he took it up to the loft. There he found that Heidi had contrived a neat little bed. At one end, where her head would rest, the hay was packed higher, and in such a way that her face would look directly towards the glassless skylight.

"You've made a fine job of this," said Grandfather, "and now for the sheet. But wait…" And he took a few more armfuls of hay from the pile and made the bed twice as deep, so that she would not feel the hard floor beneath it. "Now bring it here." Heidi quickly went to pick up the sheet, but it was so heavy she could scarcely carry it. This was no bad thing, though, as it meant the material was too thick for the sharp blades of hay to prick her through it. Together they spread the sheet over the bed, and where it hung over the sides and ends Heidi briskly tucked it under the hay. It now looked clean and tidy.

Heidi stood and pondered their handiwork for a second, then said, "We've forgotten something, Grandfather."

"What's that?" he asked.

"A cover. When you go to bed, you crawl between the sheet and the cover."

"Really? What if I haven't got one?"

"Oh, it doesn't matter, Grandfather," Heidi reassured him. "In that case I'll just use hay as a cover." Quickly she turned back to the pile of hay, but the old man stopped her.

"Wait a minute," he said, and he went down the ladder and over to his bed. He returned with a large, heavy linen sack, which he laid on the ground.

"This is better than hay, isn't it?"

Heidi picked and pulled at the sack with all her might, trying to unfold it, but its weight was too much for her small hands. Grandfather helped her, and once it was spread over the sheet the bed looked very good and well put together. Heidi stood marvelling at it and said, "That's a wonderful cover, and the bed is perfect now! I wish it was night already so I could lie in it."

"I think we might have something to eat first," said Grandfather. "Don't you?"

In her enthusiasm to make up her bed, Heidi had forgotten everything else, but at the mention of eating she felt pangs of hunger. Nothing had passed her lips since a piece of bread and a small cup of weak coffee early that morning ahead of her long journey. So she replied whole-heartedly: "Yes, I think so too."

"You go first, then, if we're agreed on that," he said, and he followed her down the ladder.

The old man went over to the stove, pushed away the large pot and pulled out a smaller one attached to a chain. He perched on a three-legged wooden stool with a round seat and blew the flames into life. While the pot was coming to the boil, he held a large piece of cheese over the fire on a long iron fork and turned it this way and that until it was golden yellow all over. Heidi watched what he did keenly. An idea must have popped into her head, for all of a sudden she sprang across to the cupboard, came back again, and then returned to it several more times. When Grandfather came to the table with a jug of milk and the fork with toasted cheese, he found the round loaf, two plates and two knives already neatly set out. Heidi had noticed them stowed in the cupboard and knew they would be needed for their meal.

"It's good that you can think for yourself," said Grandfather as he arranged the toasted cheese on pieces of bread, "but there's still something missing from the table."

Heidi saw how appetizingly the steam rose from the jug and ran back to the cupboard. There was only one little bowl, and for a second she was at a loss, but then she saw two glasses behind it. She returned in an instant and placed the bowl and one glass on the table.

"Good – you've got initiative. Now, where are you going to sit?" Grandfather occupied the only chair, so Heidi darted over to the stove, carried back the three-legged stool and sat down.

"Now you've got a seat, it's true, but it's too low," he went on, "and mine isn't high enough for you to reach the table either. But you really ought to get something inside you. Look here!" And he got up, filled the bowl with milk and set it down on his chair, which he then moved up close to the stool to provide Heidi with a table. He placed a large hunk of bread and a piece of the golden cheese there too and said, "Now, eat up!" He himself sat on a corner of the table and began his own midday meal. Heidi, whose powerful thirst during the long journey had now returned, seized her bowl and drank and drank without pausing for air. Then she took a deep breath and put the bowl down.

"Is the milk good?" asked Grandfather.

"The best I've ever drunk," Heidi answered.

"You must have some more, then." And Grandfather refilled the bowl to the brim and placed it before the girl. She bit gaily into the bread, on which she had spread some of the cheese, soft as butter after its toasting, and the two combined to make a good strong flavour. In between bites, she drank her milk and looked the picture of contentment. Once the meal was over, Grandfather went outside to put the goat pen in good order, and Heidi looked on attentively as he swept it with a broom and spread fresh straw for the animals to sleep on. Then he went into the shed next to the pen, where he sawed a rod into lengths and carved a flat section with holes to fit them into. The result, when he stood it up, looked like his own chair, only much taller. Heidi stared at it, speechless with amazement.

"Do you know what it is, Heidi?" Grandfather asked.

"It's my chair, because it's so high. You made it in no time!" she said, still full of surprise and admiration.

"She has eyes in her head, this girl, and knows what's going on around her," Grandfather murmured to himself as he went about the cottage driving in nails here and there and then repairing part of the door. He wandered from one spot to another with his hammer, nails and bits of wood, adding, mending and removing as required. Heidi followed him step by step, her eyes fixed unerringly on what he was doing, and none of it failed to interest her.

Evening came. The rustling in the old firs increased, and a powerful wind blew across and hissed and blustered through the dense treetops. The sound brought a thrill to Heidi's heart, and she skipped and leapt about under the trees in a mood of high merriment, like someone who has experienced an unknown pleasure. Grandfather was standing in the doorway of the shed watching her when they both heard a high-pitched whistle. Heidi ceased her frolics and Grandfather stepped outside. From the higher slopes goat after goat came bounding down, as if chasing one another, with Peter in their midst. Heidi shot right into the herd with a joyful cry and greeted her old friends of the morning one by one. On reaching the cottage they all halted, and two pretty, slender goats – one white, one brown – left the others. They went up to Grandfather and licked his hands, which held the salt he had ready for them every evening. While Peter made off with the rest of his troop, Heidi tenderly stroked the two goats in turn. Then she whisked round to stroke them on their other sides, and was lost in her delight at the little creatures.

"Are they ours, Grandfather? Both of them? Do they go in the pen? Will they always stay with us?" In her happiness, Heidi's questions came tumbling out, and Grandfather hardly had a chance to put in his "Yes, yes!" between one and the next. Once the goats had licked up all their salt the old man said, "Go inside and fetch your bowl and the bread!"

Heidi did so and came straight back. Grandfather milked enough from the white goat to fill the bowl and cut off a piece of bread: "Eat that and then off you go to bed! Your Aunt Dete has left another bundle for you with chemises and the like, and it's at the bottom of the cupboard if you need it. I must take the goats in now, so sleep well!"

"Goodnight, Grandfather, goodnight! But what are their names, Grandfather, what are their names?" she cried, and ran after the old man as he retreated with the goats.

"The white one is Cygnet, and the brown one is Little Bear," came the reply.

"Goodnight, Cygnet! Goodnight, Little Bear!" said Heidi, raising her voice as they both disappeared into the pen. Then she sat on the bench to eat her bread and drink her milk. The strong wind nearly blew her away, so she hurried to finish, went inside and climbed up to bed. Here she slept as blissfully as she would have done in a bed fit for a king.

Shortly afterwards, before it was completely dark, Grandfather went to bed too, for in the mornings he was always out of doors at sunrise, which broke over the mountains very early in the summer months. In the night the wind gained such force that its gusts made the whole cottage tremble and the beams creak. It howled down the chimney and wailed like the voices of lost souls, and out among the old firs it raged so mightily that a few branches crashed down.

In the middle of the night, Grandfather got up. "She's likely to be frightened," he said under his breath. He went up the ladder and over to Heidi's bed. One moment the moon was shining brightly in the sky, then clouds chased across its face and all was black again. Now the moonlight came through the round skylight and directly illuminated Heidi's bed. As she slept under the heavy cover, her cheeks were a deep red and, with her head resting tranquilly on her plump little arm, her face appeared so cheerful that she must have been dreaming of something pleasant. The old man kept his gaze on the peacefully sleeping child till the moon vanished behind the clouds again and darkness returned. Then he went back to his bed.

Chapter 3

On the Pastureland

HEIDI WAS WOKEN EARLY the next morning by a loud whistle, and on opening her eyes she saw a golden ray of sunshine stream in through the skylight onto her bed and the pile of hay beside it, illuminating the entire space with a warm glow. Heidi looked around in bewilderment and could not think where she was. Then she heard Grandfather's deep voice outside and everything came back to her: the journey she had made and her now being high up the mountain with Grandfather and no longer with old Ursel, who was very deaf and felt the cold so much that she always sat by the kitchen oven or the sitting-room stove. Heidi had had to sit there too, or at least near at hand – where the old woman, unable to hear her, could at least see her – and sometimes she had felt cramped indoors and longed to be in the open air. So on waking in her new home she was delighted to recall everything she had seen the day before and would see again – above all Cygnet and Little Bear. Heidi jumped out of bed and hastily pulled on the few items of clothing she had worn the previous day. Then she clambered down the ladder and burst out of the cottage. Peter was already there with his herd, and Grandfather was just leading Cygnet and Little Bear out of their pen so they could join the others. Heidi ran forward to bid him and the goats a good morning.

"Do you want to go with Peter to graze the goats?" asked Grandfather. Heidi leapt for joy at this suggestion. "But first wash yourself clean; otherwise the sun in the sky will laugh as it shines in its splendour and sees how grubby you are. There, it's all set up for you." He pointed to a large tub full of water that stood by the door in the sun. Heidi ran over to it and splashed and scrubbed herself until she was spotless.

Meanwhile, Grandfather entered the cottage and called back to Peter: "Come inside, goat commander, and bring your haversack with you!" A bemused Peter did as he was bidden and presented his little haversack, in which he carried his meagre midday meal. "Open it!" the old man ordered, and he placed a large piece of bread and an equally large piece of cheese inside. In his astonishment Peter opened his round eyes as wide as possible, for this was more than double the quantity of bread and cheese he already had. "Now, put this bowl in there too," the Alp Uncle went on. "The girl can't drink straight from the goat like you – she doesn't know how. So you milk her two bowlfuls at midday, because she's going up and will stay with you till you come back down. Take care she doesn't fall off any crags, you hear?"

Just then Heidi came running in. "The sun can't laugh at me now, can it, Grandfather?" she asked urgently. In her terror of the sun's mockery she had taken the rough towel he had hung next to the tub and rubbed her face, neck and arms so hard that she now stood before him as red as a lobster.

"No, there's nothing for it to laugh at now," he assured her with a smile. "But I tell you what – this evening, when you come home, you'll get yourself entirely in the tub like a fish, because if you run about like the goats you'll have black feet. Now you can both be off."

They set out for the pasture in high spirits. The wind had blown away every last wisp of cloud during the night, and a deep-blue sky now looked down on them from every side. In its midst the bright sun shimmered over the green slopes of the alps, so that all the little yellow and blue flowers opened their throats and cheerfully returned its gaze. Heidi flew this way and that and shouted for pleasure as she caught sight of an array of delicate red cowslips in one spot, then a striking blue haze of pretty gentians in another, while everywhere the golden, tender-leafed rock roses smiled and nodded in the sun. In her rapture over the countless swaying, glinting flowers, Heidi even forgot the goats, and Peter too. She bounded ahead and then off to the side, tempted on by flashes of red and yellow. At every turn she gathered masses of flowers and packed them in her apron, having decided to take them all home and stick them in the hay in her bedroom so it would look just the same as out here.

On this day Peter had to watch the goats with special care, for they imitated Heidi by running off in all directions, and as his round eyes were not adept at switching rapidly from side to side he had more work than he could well cope with. Again and again he had to whistle and call and wave his switch to drive the scattered company back together.

"Where have you got to now, Heidi?" he shouted crossly.

"Here," replied a voice from somewhere. Peter could not see her because she was sitting behind a bank thickly covered with self-heals. The air was filled with their scent, and Heidi, who had never smelt anything so delicious, had sat down among them and was inhaling their fragrance in deep gulps.

"Follow me!" cried Peter. "You mustn't fall off any crags. The Alp Uncle said so."

"Where are the crags?" asked Heidi, but she stayed where she was, for with each breath of air the sweet scent blew more strongly over her.

"Up there, right up there. We still have a long way to go, so come on now! The old eagle sits at the very top and screeches."

That had its effect. Heidi shot to her feet and ran with her apron filled with flowers towards Peter.

"You've got enough now," he said, as they continued the climb together. "Otherwise you'll keep stopping, and if you take them all there'll be none left for tomorrow."

This last point carried some force with Heidi, who did indeed want to pick more the next day. Besides, she had so many that her apron was bulging. So she walked on with Peter, and the goats moved in better order too, for they could already smell the delicious herbs on a higher grassy slope and pressed forward without pausing. This pastureland, where Peter usually halted with his goats and settled himself for the day, lay at the foot of tall cliffs that were blanketed at their base by bushes and fir trees and, farther up, reached bare and rugged into the sky. On one side were deep clefts in the rock, and Grandfather had been right to warn them. Once they had ascended to this point, Peter eased off his haversack and placed it carefully in a little hollow in the ground, knowing that the wind sometimes gusted across powerfully and not wanting to see his precious belongings bowl down the mountainside. Then he lay down with his arms and legs splayed on the sun-drenched grass to recover from the strenuous climb.

Heidi, having untied her apron, rolled it up nice and tight with the flowers inside and placed it in the hollow next to Peter's haversack. Now she sat down next to his sprawling body and looked around. The valley lay far beneath them in the dazzling morning sun. In front of her Heidi saw a large white snowfield extending right up to the deep-blue sky, and to the left a great cliff face. On all sides bare, jagged rocks rose steeply to the trees and stared down solemnly at the little girl. She sat as quiet as a mouse and cast her eyes around – near and far was deep silence, with only the wind brushing softly past the tender bluebells and the gleaming golden rock roses that grew all about and bobbed to and fro in gentle merriment on their thin stalks. Peter had fallen asleep after his exertions, and the goats clambered among the bushes higher up. Heidi had never felt so happy in her life. She drank in the golden sunlight, the fresh breezes and the delicate scent of the flowers, and she desired nothing more than to stay there for ever. Time went by, and Heidi gazed up at the many distant peaks so long and hard that they seemed to acquire faces and look upon her familiarly like old friends.

Next Heidi heard loud, harsh screeches overhead, and as she looked up a bird, larger than any she had ever seen, circled in the air with huge outspread wings, returning from each circuit to the same spot above her and uttering piercing cries.

"Peter, Peter, wake up!" shouted Heidi. "Look, it's the eagle! Look!"

Peter raised himself up and followed the bird with his eyes as it soared higher and higher into the azure sky and eventually disappeared across the grey mass of rock.

"Where's he going now?" asked Heidi, who had kept her eager eyes fixed on the bird throughout.

"Back to his nest" was Peter's answer.

"Does he live up there? How wonderful to be so high up! Why does he make that noise?"

"He can't help it."

"Let's climb up there and see where he lives," Heidi proposed.

"Oh no! Oh no!" retorted Peter, his disapproval growing with each syllable. "Even the goats can't get up there, and the Alp Uncle said you weren't to fall off any crags!"

Abruptly Peter began to whistle and call with such vigour that Heidi was at a loss to know the meaning of it. But the goats clearly understood his signals, and they bounded towards him one after another until the whole herd was assembled on the green slope. Some continued nibbling juicy stems; others raced up and down or amused themselves by butting one another with their horns. Heidi sprang to her feet and ran round among them, hugely entertained by the novel spectacle of the animals playing gaily and skipping across each other's paths. She jumped from goat to goat, getting to know each one personally and discovering their individual features and mannerisms.

As she did so, Peter fetched his haversack and set out the four portions it contained neatly in a square on the ground. The two larger portions were on Heidi's side, the smaller on his own, for he knew exactly how they had been given to him. He then took the bowl and drew good, fresh milk from Cygnet into it before setting it down in the middle of the square. He called Heidi over, but she was slower to respond than the goats had been, as she was so enchanted by the various leaps and antics of her new playmates that she had eyes and ears for nothing else. But Peter knew how to make himself heard, yelling so loud that his voice resonated all the way up the cliffs. Heidi duly appeared, and the spread looked so inviting that she danced around it with pleasure.

"Stop jigging about. It's time to eat," said Peter. "Sit down and tuck in."

Heidi sat down. "Is this milk for me?" she asked, feasting her eyes again on the prettily arranged square and its centrepiece.

"Yes," he replied, "and the bigger pieces of food are yours too, and when you've finished the milk you'll get another bowlful from Cygnet. Then it's my turn."

"And which one do you get your milk from?"

"From Dapple, my own goat. Now do tuck in!" Peter admonished her again.

Heidi drank her milk, and when she put down the empty bowl Peter got up and refilled it. As he did so, she tore off a piece from her hunk of bread and handed Peter the remainder, which was still larger than his portion, together with the whole of her big chunk of cheese.

"You have this. I've got enough."

Peter, who had almost finished his own food, looked at her in silent amazement. Never in his life could he have spoken or acted that way. At first he hesitated, unable to believe that Heidi meant what she said, but she kept holding the food out to him, and as he did not take it she laid it on his knees. Now the boy understood she was in earnest, and he took up the gift, nodded his grateful acceptance and partook of a more plentiful midday meal than any before in his years as a goatherd. As he ate, Heidi cast her eyes over the goats.

"What are they all called, Peter?" she enquired.

This information he could give without difficulty, safely stored as it was in his head alongside not much else. Without further prodding, he went through all the names, identifying the animal that bore each one with his finger.

Heidi attended closely to what he said, and before long she could tell the goats apart and call them by name, for they all had peculiarities that could not fail to stick in her mind. One only needed to watch them closely, and this Heidi did.

First there was Turk, a big animal with powerful horns that liked nothing better than butting these against the other goats, which mostly ran off at his approach and wanted nothing to do with such a ruffian. The only one not to cede his ground was the jaunty Thistle Finch, a small, slender goat with a loud bleat, who would rush at Turk three or four times in quick succession. He did this in such a bold, warlike way, and possessed such sharp little horns, that the larger goat often halted in astonishment and gave up his attack. Then there was Snow Hop, small and white, who kept crying out so piteously that Heidi was forever running over and cradling her head to comfort her. Now again the girl raced up in response to an appeal from the same plaintive young voice. She wrapped a sympathetic arm round the goat's neck and asked, "What's the matter, Snow Hop? Why are you calling for help?" Trustingly the little creature nestled up to Heidi and fell silent.

From where he sat Peter shouted across to her – with interruptions for biting and swallowing: "She's doing that because the old girl has gone. She was sold the day before yesterday in Maienfeld, so she won't be coming up to pasture any more."

"What old girl?" Heidi asked.

"Her mother, of course."

"Where's her grandmother?"

"Hasn't got one."

"And a grandfather?"

"No."

"Ah, you poor little Snow Hop!" said Heidi, pressing herself tenderly against the animal. "But look, don't wail any more. I'll come with you every day and you won't be so alone, and if anything is the matter you can come to me."

Snow Hop contentedly rubbed her head against Heidi's shoulder and stopped her wretched bleating. Meanwhile, Peter, having finished his meal, walked over to his herd and to Heidi, who was once more observing the goats closely. By far the prettiest and cleanest of the whole group were Cygnet and Little Bear, who also had a certain refinement of bearing, kept mostly to themselves and in particular stayed contemptuously aloof from the intrusive Turk.

The goats were now starting to climb up to the bushes again, and each had its own manner of doing so. Some pranced lightly over all obstacles, others searched unhurriedly for tasty plants to eat on the way, and Turk looked for opportunities for his attacks. Cygnet and Little Bear moved ahead with nimble elegance, and once on the higher ground they quickly found the finest bushes, positioned themselves with skill on their hind legs and nibbled daintily at the leaves. Heidi stood with her hands on her hips and surveyed the scene with rapt attention.

"Peter," she remarked to the boy, once again flat on his back, "the best-looking of all are Cygnet and Little Bear."

"I know," was his reply. "The Alp Uncle washes and brushes them and gives them salt and has the best pen."

All of a sudden Peter jumped up and made off towards the goats in leaps and bounds, with Heidi hard on his heels. Something must have happened, and she did not want to stay behind. Peter ran right through the herd to the side of the pastureland that ended in a sheer drop down bare rock, so that if a goat heedlessly strayed too far this way it could fall off the edge and break all its legs. He had spotted Thistle Finch hopping over to that side and arrived just in time, for the inquisitive creature was rapidly nearing the precipice. To catch him he dived to the ground and just managed to seize one of his hind legs. Thistle Finch bleated in angry surprise at being prevented from continuing his merry course and stubbornly tried to pull his leg free of Peter's grasp. Unable to get up and almost yanking the goat's leg from its socket, the boy called out to Heidi for help. She was there in a flash, and immediately saw the peril both were in. Hastily she pulled a few sweet-smelling plants out of the ground and held them under the animal's nose.

"Come on, Thistle Finch, come on," she said soothingly. "Why don't you be sensible? Look, you could fall over the edge and break a leg, and that would be so painful."

In no time the young goat turned round and blithely devoured the plants in Heidi's hand. Then Peter, having got to his feet, grasped the cord round Thistle Finch's neck to which his bell was attached. Heidi took hold of the cord on the other side, and they guided the runaway back to the peacefully grazing herd. Once he was in safety, Peter raised his switch to give him a good beating in punishment, and Thistle Finch, sensing what was coming, shrank back in fear. But Heidi cried out, "No, Peter, no! Don't hit him. Look how frightened he is!"

"Serves him right," growled Peter, about to strike.

But Heidi fell against his arm and shouted indignantly, "You mustn't! You'll hurt him. Leave him alone!"

Peter looked in wonder at the commanding figure of Heidi, whose flashing black eyes somehow forced him to lower his switch.

Having relented, he wanted some compensation for the shock he had received: "I'll let him off if you give me some of your cheese again tomorrow."

"You can have it all, the whole piece, tomorrow and every day," Heidi assented. "I can easily do without it. And I'll give you as much bread as I did today. But then you must never ever beat Thistle Finch, or Snow Hop, or any of the other goats."

"All the same to me," he replied, which was his way of agreeing to the bargain. Peter now let loose the culprit, who joyfully kicked up his heels and bolted off to the herd.

The hours fled by, and the sun was about to sink beneath the distant peaks. Heidi sat on the ground again and silently contemplated the bluebells and rock roses as they shone in the golden evening light, and all the grass was tinged with gold too, while the crags began to glimmer and sparkle. Suddenly Heidi sprang to her feet.

"Peter! Peter!" she screamed. "There's a fire, a fire! All the mountains are burning, and all the snow over there and the sky. Oh, look, look: the great bare peak is glowing! How beautiful the fiery snow is! Peter, stand up and look – the fire has reached up to where the eagle lives. Look at the crags, and at the firs. Everything is on fire!"

"It's always like that," said Peter unmoved, and went on filing his stick, "but it isn't really fire."

"What is it, then?" asked Heidi as she jumped from one spot to another to get the best view. There was so much beauty on all sides that she could not tire of it. "What is it, Peter, what is it?"

"It happens by itself," he explained.

"Oh, look, look!" shouted Heidi excitedly. "Now the mountains are turning red. See the one covered in snow and the high one with the jagged face! What are they called, Peter?"

"Mountains don't have names."

"How lovely they are! See how red the snow is. And it looks like those crags are covered all over with roses. Now they're turning grey. Oh no, it's all snuffed out! Peter, it's all gone!" And Heidi sat on the ground and looked as distraught as she well might at the idea of the crimson twilight lost for ever.

"It'll be the same tomorrow," Peter told her. "Stand up, now. We must get home." He whistled and called his goats together, and they set off on their return journey.

"Is it always just like this, every day when we bring the goats up to graze?" asked Heidi as she walked at Peter's side down the pastureland. Eagerly she waited for his reassurance that it was so.

"Most days," he replied.

"What about tomorrow?" she wanted to know.

"Tomorrow yes."

This made Heidi happy again. She had collected so many new impressions and there were so many thoughts racing through her brain that she said nothing until they reached Grandfather's cottage and saw him sitting under the fir trees. Since the goats always came down on this side, the old man had placed a bench there so that he could sit and wait for them every evening. Heidi dashed over to him, with Cygnet and Little Bear, who knew their master and their pen, close behind.

Peter called after Heidi, "Goodnight! Come tomorrow too!" He was very anxious that Heidi should accompany him again.

Heidi ran straight back to give him her hand and promise that she would do so. Then she leapt right into the herd as it was moving off and clasped her arms round Snow Hop's neck.

"Sleep well, Snow Hop," she said confidingly, "and remember I'll be coming again tomorrow and you needn't bleat in such a sad way any more."

The goat beamed at her in gratitude and then scampered off after the others, while Heidi went back under the firs.

"Oh Grandfather, it was so nice!" she exclaimed before she had even reached him. "The fire and the roses on the crags and the blue and yellow flowers. And look what I've brought you!" From her folded apron she shook out the profusion of flowers for him to see – but what a sight the poor flowers were! Heidi did not recognize them. They looked like hay, not a single one with its cup open. "Oh Grandfather, what's the matter with them?" cried the startled girl. "This isn't how they were. Why do they look like this?"

"They want to stand outside in the sun, not be tucked up in an apron," he said.

"Then I won't bring any more. But Grandfather, why did the eagle screech so?" Heidi asked urgently.

"First have a bath while I go to the pen to get some milk. After that we'll meet in the cottage for our evening meal, and then I'll tell you."

She took her bath, and later, as she perched on her tall chair with a bowl of milk before her and the old man beside her, the child repeated her question: "Grandfather, why does the eagle screech so and call down to the ground?"

"He's mocking the people below because they huddle together in villages and get on each other's nerves. He's saying: 'If you would only go your separate ways and rise up to the heights as I have, you'd all be better off!'" Grandfather's voice was almost savage as he spoke these words, which made the eagle's screeches seem even more impressive in Heidi's recollection.

"Grandfather, why don't the mountains have names?" was Heidi's next question.

"They do have names," he replied, "and if you describe one to me and I recognize it I'll tell you what it's called."

Heidi described the craggy mountain with the twin peaks exactly as it had looked to her, and Grandfather said with satisfaction, "Very well, I know the one – it's the Falknis. Did you see any others?"

Now she told him of the mountain with the great snow-field, and how all the snow had been on fire and then turned reddish, and then in a few seconds the colour had faded to nothing.

"That one I know too. It's the Schesaplana. So you enjoyed taking the goats up to graze?"

Heidi gave him an account of the whole day and how lovely it had been, especially the fire in the evening, and she asked Grandfather to tell her what caused the fire, for Peter had known nothing about it.

"Well, it's the sun, you see," he answered. "As it says goodnight to the mountains, it casts its most beautiful rays over them so they don't forget it in the hours before it rises again in the morning."

This captivated Heidi, and she longed for the arrival of the next day, when she would be able to go up to the pastureland and again watch the sun bidding the mountains goodnight. But first she had to sleep, and on her bed of hay she slept wonderfully well the whole night through. She dreamt of shimmering mountains strewn with red roses, and among them Snow Hop joyfully running and leaping about.

Chapter 4

At Grandmother's

THE FOLLOWING MORNING was just as bright and sunny, and when Peter came with the goats the two children went together up to the pasture. So it went on day after day, and this healthy life of grazing the goats made Heidi tanned and strong. She was so content that she had nothing to wish for, and she passed her time with the same carefree merriment as the little birds thronging the trees of the green woodlands. Then autumn came and the winds whistled more noisily over the mountains, and sometimes Grandfather said, "Today you'll stay here, Heidi. A sudden gust of wind could blow a little girl like you off the edge of a cliff into the valley."

On the mornings that Peter heard him say this, he felt gloomy about the hours ahead and wore a dejected look. For one thing he was bored out of his mind when Heidi was not with him, and for another he was deprived of his abundant midday meal. Then, too, the goats were so obstinate on these days that he had twice the usual trouble with them; they had grown so used to Heidi's company that in her absence they refused to move in a straight line and instead ran off in all directions. Heidi herself always had something pleasant to look forward to and so was never unhappy. Best of all she liked to go with the goat-herd and his charges to the pasture, where the flowers, the eagle and the peculiarities of the goats offered many and varied experiences. But Grandfather's hammering and sawing and carpentering entertained her too, and if she had to stay at home on a day when he was making the fine round goat's-milk cheeses it was a special treat to watch him engaged in this curious activity. He would roll up his sleeves and stir the contents of the big pot with his bare arms.

Most appealing of all to Heidi on these windy days were the swaying and swishing of the three ancient firs behind the cottage. Whatever she was doing, she had to leave it from time to time and run there, for nothing could be as wonderful and impressive as the deep, mysterious roar in the lofty treetops. Heidi would stand below and listen carefully, and she could not get enough of seeing and hearing how the mighty element blew and heaved and whistled through the trees. Since the sun no longer gave so much heat as in the summer, Heidi sought out her stockings and shoes and also her dress. It became cooler and cooler, and when she stood under the firs the wind went through her as if she were the merest leaf. Nonetheless she kept coming back, and if she saw from the cottage that it was blowing hard she could not stay indoors.

In time it grew really cold, and Peter breathed into his hands when he came early in the mornings, until his visits came to a stop after a heavy fall of snow one night. The following morning the whole pasture was white, with not a single green leaf as far as the eye could see. Neither goatherd nor goats appeared, and Heidi peered in wonder through a small window as the snow started to come down again. The thick flakes fell and fell until the snow reached right up the windows, and then higher still so that they were stuck fast and she and Grandfather were sealed up in the little house. This seemed such fun to Heidi that she ran from window to window to see how much more snow would come down, and whether it would cover the whole cottage and oblige them to use a lamp in the middle of the day.

It did not come to this, and on the next day, the snowfall having ceased, Grandfather went outside and cleared all round the cottage with his shovel, building up huge piles of snow that looked like mountains around their home. Now the windows could be opened and the door too. This was a good thing, for as Heidi and Grandfather were seated by the fire in the afternoon, each on a three-legged stool – he having long since made one for her too – something thundered up to the cottage, banged repeatedly against the wooden threshold and at last opened the door. There stood Peter, but it was not rudeness that had made him pound on the door, rather he had been kicking the snow off his boots, which had been encased in it all the way up. Indeed the boy was covered with snow from head to foot, having fought his way through the deep drifts and broken off chunks that stuck to his clothes as they froze in the biting cold. He had not given up, though, because he had not seen Heidi for eight days and was determined to reach the cottage.

On entering, he said, "Good afternoon," and placed himself as near to the fire as he could. He said nothing further, but his whole face beamed with delight that he had made it. Heidi looked at him with great surprise, for he was so close to the fire that everything began to melt around him and his whole body resembled a gentle cascade.

"Well, commander, how are things?" asked Grandfather. "You've got no troops under you now and have to chew on your pencil instead."

"Why does he have to chew on his pencil, Grandfather?" Heidi broke in, anxious to understand.

"In winter he has to go to school," Grandfather told her, "where you learn to read and write. That's no easy matter, and sometimes it helps a little if you chew on your pencil – isn't that so, commander?"

"It is," Peter confirmed.

This awakened Heidi's interest in the topic, and she asked Peter a great many questions about school and what you could see, hear and experience there. Since any conversation involving Peter was bound to progress slowly, he was nice and dry all over by the time it finished. He always struggled to put his thoughts into the right words, and now the task was especially hard, because as soon as he produced one answer Heidi threw two or three more unexpected questions at him, mostly ones that called for a full sentence in response. Grandfather remained silent during this exchange, but a repeated twitch at the corner of his mouth indicated that he was listening with amusement.

"Well, commander, you've been in the line of fire and need some sustenance. So come on!" With these words the old man got up and fetched the evening meal from the cupboard, while Heidi arranged the chairs round the table. There was now also a bench against the wall that Grandfather had carpentered and secured there. Since Heidi's arrival he had made seats big enough for two in various places, for she was in the habit of staying close to him wherever he went and stood or sat, and as a result there was plenty of seating for all three of them. Peter opened his round eyes very wide when he saw what a huge portion of the delicious smoked ham the Alp Uncle placed on his thick slice of bread. He had not eaten so well in a long while. Once the cheerful meal was over, it began to grow dark and Peter made ready to set off for home. After thanking them and bidding them goodnight, he turned round in the doorway and said to Heidi: "I'll come again next Sunday, a week from today, and Grandmother said that you should visit her one day too."

The idea that she should pay someone a visit was a new one for Heidi, but it quickly took root in her mind, and the next morning her first words were: "Grandfather, I must go down to Peter's grandmother now. She's expecting me."

"There's too much snow," he countered. But Heidi did not give up her intention; the grandmother had sent word for her to come, and come she must. Each day that passed she said half a dozen times, "Grandfather, it's really time I went to the grandmother. She's waiting for me."

On the fourth day – when the great blanket of snow all around had frozen solid and every step outdoors created a grating, crunching sound, but a bright sun gazed in through the window straight at the tall chair on which Heidi ate her midday meal – she again returned to her theme: "Today I really must go to the grandmother, or she'll think it's too long."

At this Grandfather rose from the table, climbed up to the hayloft and brought down the thick sacking that was Heidi's bedcover.

"Come on, then!" he said.

The enraptured girl skipped after him into the glittering white world outside. The ancient firs were quite still, their boughs heavy with snow, and the sun made them shimmer and sparkle so magnificently that Heidi leapt into the air with delight. Again and again she cried, "Come out, Grandfather, come out! There's gold and silver all over the firs!"

The old man had gone into the shed, and now he emerged with a broad sledge. To one side a rail was attached, and from the flat seat the rider could extend his legs forward and stem his feet against the snow, using one or the other to steer. After acceding to Heidi's wish that they have a good look at the firs, Grandfather sat on the sledge and took the child in his lap, wrapped the sacking round and round her to keep her nice and warm and pressed her against himself with his left arm, an important precaution for the journey ahead. Then he took hold of the rail with his right hand and pushed off with both feet. The sledge shot down the mountainside at such a pace that Heidi thought it was flying through the air like a bird and screamed with delight. All at once they came to a standstill next to Peter's cottage. The old man set the girl on her feet and removed her wrap.

"Now go in," he said, "and when it starts to get dark come out again and make your way home." He then turned back up the mountain, pulling his sledge after him.

Heidi opened the door and entered a small, dark room with a stove and a few dishes in a rack. This was the kitchen, and from it she opened a second door that led into a poky sitting room. Unlike Grandfather's typical Alpine cottage, made up of a single large room with a hayloft above, this was a tiny, very old house in which everything was mean and cramped. Stepping into the sitting room, Heidi found herself right in front of a table, and seated there was a woman mending what she instantly recognized to be Peter's jacket. In the corner a small, bent old woman sat before a spinning wheel. Heidi did not need to be told who was who. She went directly to the old woman and said, "Good day, Grandmother. I'm here. I hope you don't think I was too long coming?"

Raising her head, Grandmother felt for the hand that was held out to her, and once she had grasped it in her own she stroked it pensively for a few moments. Then she said, "Are you Heidi, the girl who lives up with the Alp Uncle?"

"Yes I am," Heidi confirmed, "and I have just ridden down on the sledge with him."

"How can that be? Your hand is so warm. Brigitte, did the Alp Uncle bring the child himself?"

Peter's mother had put aside her work and risen from the table. She looked the girl up and down with curiosity and then replied, "I don't know if he brought her himself, Mother. It seems hard to believe – most likely the child is mistaken."

Heidi looked at the younger woman resolutely, without a trace of uncertainty, and said, "I know very well who wrapped me in the bedcover and came down with me on the sledge. It was Grandfather."

"There must be some truth in what Peter was saying over the summer about the Alp Uncle, when we thought he didn't know what he was talking about," said Grandmother. "But who would have thought it possible? I didn't think the child would stick it out three weeks up there! How does she look, Brigitte?"

Brigitte studied Heidi from all sides so that she could report on her appearance. "She's small-boned, as Adelheid was," she replied, "but she's got black eyes and curly hair, just like Tobias and the old man too. She takes more after them, I think."

Meanwhile Heidi was not idle. She trained her eyes keenly round the room and took everything in. Then she said, "Look, Grandmother, that shutter there is banging to and fro. Grandfather would knock in a nail in no time to hold it in place. Otherwise it will break the glass one day. Just look at it now!"

"You're a good girl," said the old woman. "I can't see it, but I can hear it well enough – and many other things too, not just the shutter. On a windy day everything creaks and rattles, and the draughts get in on all sides. The whole place is coming apart, and at night, when the other two are asleep, I'm sometimes scared stiff that it will fall down and kill us all. And there's no one here who can make repairs. Peter doesn't know how."

"But why can't you see the shutter, Grandmother? Look, there it goes again, just there." Heidi indicated the spot clearly with her finger.

"Dear girl, it isn't just the shutter I can't see. I can't see anything at all," said Grandmother sadly.

"But if I go outside and open the shutter fully so all the light comes in, will you see then, Grandmother?"

"No, not even then. Nobody can make it light for me now."

"What if you go outside into the pure white snow? You must be able to see something then. Just come with me, Grandmother, and I'll show you." Heidi took the old woman's hand and wanted to lead her from her seat, for she was growing alarmed at the idea of her not seeing at all.

"You're a kind girl, but leave me be. My world will stay dark, even outside in the snow. The light doesn't reach my eyes any more."

"Surely in the summer it will, Grandmother," said Heidi, casting about in growing desperation for a solution. "You know, when the hot sun beats down and then says good-night to the mountains and they turn red like fire and the yellow flowers gleam like gold. That will make your eyes well again."

"My dear, I won't ever see the fiery mountains or the golden flowers again. The light has gone out of my life for good."

Heidi broke out in sobs, and in her distress she could not stop her tears: "Who can make you see again? Can't anyone? Anyone at all?"

Grandmother tried to console the child, but it was no easy task. Heidi almost never cried, but once she started she found it hard to overcome her sadness. Grandmother's heart was wrung by such pitiful sobbing, and she tried various ways of pacifying her. At last she said, "Now, now, my dear Heidi, come here. I've got something to tell you. Look, if someone can't see it's even nicer to hear a friendly voice, and I'd like to hear you speak. So come and sit by me and tell me a bit about how you live up there with your grandfather and how he fills his time. I used to know him well, but for years I've heard nothing of him except what Peter says, and that isn't much."

At this moment an idea occurred to Heidi, and quickly she wiped away her tears. "Just wait, Grandmother," she said comfortingly. "I'll tell Grandfather everything, and he'll give you your sight back and make sure your cottage doesn't fall down. He can put all things right."

The old woman did not reply, so Heidi began in a lively voice to tell her about her life with Grandfather and the days on the pastureland and their present winter activities, and how Grandfather could make all sorts of things out of wood: benches and chairs, cribs to fill with hay for Cygnet and Little Bear, a big new water trough for summer bathing and a new milk bowl and spoons. She grew quite ardent as she described the beautiful things that so rapidly took shape from blocks of wood, and how she would stand next to Grandfather and watch him, and how she hoped to make similar things herself one day.

Grandmother listened closely, and now and again she remarked, "Did you hear that, Brigitte? Do you hear what she's saying about the Alp Uncle?"

Suddenly Heidi's account was interrupted by loud noises outside the door, and then Peter stomped into the room. He pulled up short and opened his round eyes exceedingly wide when he saw Heidi. She called out, "Hello, Peter," and his face creased into the friendliest of smiles.

"Can he really be home from school already?" exclaimed Grandmother, quite taken aback. "I haven't known an afternoon go by so quickly in years! Hello, Peter dear, how's the reading going?"

"Just the same."

"Ah well," said Grandmother with a gentle sigh. "I thought things might change with time – you'll be twelve years old in February."

This sparked Heidi's interest. "Why should things change with time?" she asked.

"I only meant he might have made progress with it," Grandmother replied. "With reading, that is. Up on that shelf I've got an old prayer book, and in it are some beautiful hymns that I haven't heard for a long time, and I can't recite them from memory either. So I kept hoping that if Peter learnt his letters he might read one to me now and then. But he can't master it – it's too hard for him."

"I think I'll have to light the lamp. It's getting quite dark already," said Peter's mother, who was still busily mending his jacket. "I don't know where the time has gone this afternoon either."

At this Heidi jumped up from her low chair, hastily extended her hand and said, "Goodnight, Grandmother. I must go home as soon as it gets dark." And, having shaken hands with Peter and his mother, she made for the door.

But Grandmother called out anxiously, "Wait, wait, Heidi. You can't go alone. Peter must go with you, do you hear? And take care of her, Peter. Don't let her fall or get cold by standing still too long, do you hear? Has she got a thick scarf on?"

"I haven't got any scarf," called back Heidi, "but I won't get cold." She was already out of the door, darting off so nimbly that Peter could scarcely keep up with her.

"Run after her, Brigitte, run," wailed Grandmother. "The child will freeze to death outside in the dark. Take my scarf and quickly run after her!"

Brigitte did so, but the children had only taken a few steps up the mountain when they saw the Alp Uncle coming down towards them. "Good girl, Heidi, you've kept your word!" he said. He wrapped her tight in the sacking, took her in his arm and began the homeward climb.

Brigitte was just in time to see the old man lift up the muffled child and set off for home. She went back in the cottage with Peter and told Grandmother with some surprise what had taken place. Grandmother was no less surprised. "Praise the Lord that he treats the child so well, praise the Lord!" she kept on saying. "If only he'll let her come down to see me again. She's done me a power of good. Such a kind heart she has, and such a pretty way of describing things!" And Grandmother dwelt with pleasure on the visit until she went to bed. "I just hope she comes again!" she said and repeated. "Now I have something in this world to look forward to after all!"

And each time Grandmother made these remarks, Brigitte chimed in with her agreement, while Peter indicated his by nodding and grinning broadly. "I knew this is how it would be," he said.

Outside, Heidi, ensconced in her sacking, was chattering away to Grandfather non-stop. But as her voice did not penetrate through the eight layers of linen he did not understand a word. "Just wait a bit till we get home, then tell me," he said.

As soon as they arrived he went indoors and unwrapped Heidi, who immediately said, "Grandfather, tomorrow we must take the hammer and the big nails down to Grandmother's and fix her shutter in place and make some other repairs too, because everything in the house creaks and rattles."

"Must we? Are you sure? Who told you so?" asked Grandfather.

"No one told me so. I know it myself," replied Heidi, "because everything is rickety, and sometimes Grandmother lies awake at night scared stiff and thinks, 'Now it will collapse on top of our heads.' And no one can make Grandmother see again – she doesn't know how anyone could – but I'm sure you could, Grandfather. Just think how sad it must be always to be in darkness and always in a fright, and there's no one who can help her except you! So let's go tomorrow. Please, Grandfather, say we can!"

Heidi clung to him and turned her face up to his with boundless trust. The old man looked down at the child for a while, and then he said, "All right, Heidi, we'll stop the rattling in Grandmother's house. That we can do, and we'll do it tomorrow."

The child skipped all round the room for joy and chanted, "We'll do it tomorrow! We'll do it tomorrow!"

Grandfather was true to his word, and the following afternoon saw them complete the same journey by sledge. Once more he set her down at the door of the goatherd's cottage and said, "Now, go inside, and when it gets dark go home again." Then he laid the sacking on the sledge and walked round the side of the little house.

No sooner had Heidi opened the door and burst into the sitting room when Grandmother cried out from her corner, "The girl has come! She's come!" In her delight she let her thread fall from one hand and the spindle from the other and extended both towards the visitor. Heidi ran across to her, quickly pushed the low chair right next to her and sat down. Once again she had a whole host of things to tell and ask her, but without warning they heard such a mighty banging against the outside of the house that Grandmother nearly jumped out of her skin and upset her spinning wheel. All atremble, she cried, "Oh my God, now it's happening. The place is falling down!"

But Heidi took her firmly by the arm and soothed her: "No, no, Grandmother, don't be frightened. It's only Grandfather with his hammer. He's mending everything so you won't need to be afraid any more."

"Well, of all the things! Of all the things in the world! It looks like the Lord hasn't forgotten us after all," exclaimed Grandmother. "Did you hear, Brigitte, did you hear what the noise is? I can tell now that it really is a hammer! Go outside, Brigitte, and if it's the Alp Uncle ask him to come in for a moment so I can thank him."

Brigitte went out and found the Alp Uncle driving new tie beams into the wall with great vigour. She approached him and said, "A good afternoon to you, Uncle, from my mother too. We're grateful to you for doing us such a kind service, and my mother would like to thank you inside. To be sure, no one else would have seen to it so quickly, and we're all the more grateful—"

"Save your breath," the old man interrupted her. "I know what you think of the Alp Uncle. Just go back inside. I'll see for myself what needs doing."

Brigitte obeyed instantly, for he had a way about him that discouraged opposition. He knocked and hammered his way all round the house, then climbed up the narrow steps to the underside of the eaves and carried on hammering until he had used every last nail he had brought with him. By this time the light was fading, and as soon as he came down and hauled the sledge out of the goat pen he saw Heidi emerge from the door. He wrapped her up as on the previous day and took her in one arm, pulling the sledge behind him, because if she had sat on it alone her covering would all have slipped off and she might have frozen to death. Knowing this, Grandfather kept the child warm in his arm.

Thus passed the winter. After many drab years a new pleasure had entered the blind grandmother's life, and her days no longer seemed so long and dark or so monotonous now that she always had something to look forward to. From early morning she listened out for the sound of tripping footsteps, and if she heard the door open and the girl rush in she would cry out in delight: "Thank the Lord, she's come again!" Heidi then sat by her and chatted merrily, telling her everything that came into her head and making the old woman feel so contented that the hours went by unnoticed. Not once did her old question, "Brigitte, isn't it evening yet?" pass her lips. Instead, when Heidi closed the door behind her, she said, "Well, Brigitte, where did the afternoon go?"

And Brigitte would reply, "I know, it seems no time at all since I put the lunch things away."

"May the good Lord protect her, and keep the Alp Uncle willing to let her come! Does she look healthy, Brigitte?"

To this the answer did not vary: "She looks like a rosy-red apple."

Heidi was quite as attached to Grandmother as Grandmother was to her, and she felt sorely grieved when she reflected that nobody, not even Grandfather, could restore her sight. Grandmother told her many times that in her company she did not mind the impairment nearly so much, and on every fine day throughout the winter Heidi made the journey down on the sledge. Grandfather continued without further explanation to bring her, and also his hammer and other tools, and often he spent his afternoons patching up the little house. As a result of his labours it ceased to creak and rattle all night long, and Grandmother said she had not slept so soundly for many a winter, and that she would never forget the Alp Uncle's good deed.

Chapter 5

Two Visitors

THE WINTER SEEMED SHORT, the cheerful summer that followed it shorter still, and now another winter was nearing its close. Heidi was as happy and chirpy as the birds in the air, and with each day her delight increased at the imminent onset of spring, when the warm föhn wind would rush through the firs and sweep away the snow, and the bright sun would tease open the little blue and yellow flowers. Then the days on the pastureland would begin, offering Heidi the greatest of her earthly pleasures. She was now in her eighth year, and had learnt all sorts of useful things from Grandfather. She could handle goats as well as anyone, and Cygnet and Little Bear followed her about like faithful poodles and bleated with joy at the mere sound of her voice.

Twice this winter Peter had brought messages from the village schoolmaster informing the Alp Uncle that he should send the child in his care to school. She was more than old enough, and ought to have attended the previous winter. On both occasions the Alp Uncle had sent word that if the schoolmaster wished to speak with him he would find him at home, and that he would not be sending the child to school. These messages Peter faithfully delivered.

In March the sun melted the snow on the slopes and snowdrops peeped though everywhere, while the boughs of the firs in the valley and on the mountainside shrugged off their white burden and swayed merrily in the breeze. Heidi was in high spirits, running back and forth between the front door and the goat pen, from there to the firs behind the cottage, and back indoors to tell Grandfather how much bigger the green patch under the trees had grown. Then she went out to have another look, for she could hardly wait for everything to be green again and for summer to spread its mantle of leaves and flowers over the pastureland.

On just such a sunny March morning Heidi was rushing about as usual, but as she leapt over the threshold to go outside for about the tenth time she started in alarm and almost fell backwards through the doorway. Before her, looking at her gravely, stood an elderly gentleman dressed in black. When he saw what a fright she had had, he said in a friendly voice, "You needn't be afraid of me – I like children. You must be Heidi – give me your hand. Where's your grandfather?"

"He's sitting at the table making spoons out of wood," Heidi told him, and she opened the door.

The visitor was the village pastor, who had known the Alp Uncle well in earlier years, when they had lived close by each other in the village. He entered the cottage and walked across to the old man, who was bent over his carving. "Good morning, neighbour," he said.

The Alp Uncle looked up in surprise, got to his feet and replied, "A good morning to you, pastor." He placed his chair in front of his guest. "If you won't shun a wooden chair, please take this one."

The pastor sat down. "It's been a long while since I last saw you, neighbour."

"Or I you," came the answer.

"I've come today to talk something over with you," the pastor went on. "I think you can guess what my business is – what I want to put to you and hear your thoughts on."

He paused and looked at the girl, who stood by the door observing him closely.

"Heidi, go out to the goats," said Grandfather. "You can take a little salt, and stay there till I come."

Heidi disappeared instantly, and the pastor resumed, "The girl should really have attended school last winter, and this winter most definitely. The schoolmaster reminded you, but you took no notice. What do you mean to do with her, neighbour?"

"I mean not to send her to school," he replied.

The visitor turned a perplexed face to the Alp Uncle, who sat on his bench with his arms stubbornly crossed.

"What do you want to make of her, then?" the pastor now asked.

"Nothing. She'll thrive growing up with the goats and the birds. With them she's happy, and she'll learn no evil from them."

"But she isn't a goat or a bird: she's a human being. And if she learns no evil from these playfellows, she'll learn nothing else either. But she needs to learn, and it's time she started. I've come to tell you now, neighbour, so you can think it over and make the necessary arrangements during the summer. The girl won't go through another winter untaught. Next winter she'll go to school, and she'll do so every day."

"I won't do it, pastor," said the old man steadfastly.

"Do you honestly think there are no means to bring you to your senses if you obstinately persist in your unreasonable conduct?" said the pastor, growing a little heated. "You've seen the world and had the opportunity to broaden your mind. I would have expected you to show more understanding, neighbour."

"Indeed," the Alp Uncle responded, his voice betraying that he too was starting to lose his cool, "and do you really think I'm going to send a slip of a girl down the mountain through snow and high winds every ice-cold morning next winter, a two-hour journey, and then back up every afternoon? The way the wind swirls around and whips up the snow is enough to knock the breath out of a grown man, let alone a child like her. And perhaps you remember Adelheid, her mother, who sometimes walked in her sleep and had queer spells. Do you want the girl to go the same way because of exhaustion? I'd like to see someone try to force my hand! I'll go to every court in the land with her, and we'll see who comes out on top!"

"You're quite right, neighbour," said the pastor genially, "it would be quite impossible to send the child to school from here. But I can see she's dear to you, so why not do something for her sake that you ought to have done long ago – come back down to the village and live among your fellow men! What kind of life is it up here, alone and embittered against God and man? And if anything should happen to you, who would come to your aid? I don't see how you can avoid half-freezing to death in this cottage during the winter, and it's a wonder that a delicate girl can stand it at all!"

"She has young blood in her veins and a good bedcover, I can assure you. And another thing: I know where to get firewood, and when it's time to lay it in. You can take a look in my shed, it's all there. The fire in this cottage doesn't go out all winter long. And what you've said about moving to the village won't do. The people down there despise me – and I them – so it's best for both sides if we keep our distance."

"No, no, it isn't best for you. I know what you're missing," said the pastor cordially. "As for people there despising you, it isn't as bad as you suppose. Trust me, neighbour, make your peace with God, ask His forgiveness if you need it, and then come and see how differently people will perceive you and how much better you'll feel!"

He stood up and offered the old man his hand, continuing in the same friendly tone, "Well, I'm counting on you to be back among us next winter, and we'll be good neighbours just as before. It would grieve me if we had to put pressure on you. So give me your hand and promise you'll come down and live among us again, reconciled with God and man!"

The Alp Uncle took the pastor's hand. His reply was firm and resolute: "You mean well by me, but I must tell you straight that I will not do as you say, nor will I change my mind. I won't send the girl to school or come to the village to live."

"Then God be with you!" said the pastor, and he made his way sadly out of the cottage and down the mountain.

He left the Alp Uncle out of sorts. In the afternoon, when Heidi pointed out it was time to go to Grandmother's, he only replied, "Not today." He said nothing more the whole of that day, and next morning, on Heidi asking if they would go to Grandmother's, his answer was equally curt: "We'll see."

Before they had even cleared the table after the midday meal, another visitor came through the door. It was Aunt Dete. She wore a smart hat with a feather and a long dress that swept everything on the cottage floor along with it, including much that had no place on the fabric of a dress. The Alp Uncle looked her up and down without saying a word. But Dete had come with the aim of having a most amicable conversation, and she launched straight into praises of Heidi's looks, saying she hardly recognized her and could easily see she had been well cared for at Grandfather's. Of course, Dete went on, she had always intended to take the girl off his hands and well understood that she must get in his way, but when she had brought her she really had nowhere else to turn. Since then she had been racking her brains day and night to think of

where she might place the girl, and that was her reason
for coming today, for out of the blue she had heard something that indicated such a rare bit of luck for Heidi that
she had almost refused to believe it. She had looked into
it directly, though, and was now able to say that it was
pretty well all true, and that the good fortune awaiting
Heidi was one in a million. An immensely rich relative of
her employers, who lived in more or less the finest house
in Frankfurt, had an only daughter who was confined to a
wheelchair because she was lame on one side and in poor
general health. For this reason she was very isolated and
had to take her lessons alone with a tutor, which she found
extremely dull. She longed for a companion for her daily
life at home, and her father, who was full of tenderness
for his ailing daughter, wanted to oblige her. His housekeeper had described to Dete's employers what kind of
companion they were seeking, and they had talked the
matter over. The housekeeper had said they were looking for a quite unspoilt child with an original way about
her, something out of the common run. Dete had herself
immediately thought of Heidi, and without delay had gone
to the housekeeper to tell her all about the girl and her
character, and the other woman had agreed on the spot.
There was no limit to the happiness and comfort Heidi
might have ahead of her, because once she got there and
if the people liked her, and if anything should happen to
the invalid daughter – and with her being so sickly you
never knew – well, the father wouldn't want to be without
a child in the house, and in that case her prospects would
be quite simply—"

"Have you nearly finished?" the Alp Uncle interrupted her, having remained silent up to this point.

"Pah," retorted Dete, tossing her head back. "You're acting as if I'd said the most commonplace thing, yet there's no one in the whole of Prättigau valley who wouldn't offer up thanks to the Lord for the news I've given you today."

"Give it to someone else, then. I'm not interested," he said drily.

At this, Dete flared up like a rocket: "Well, if that's your attitude, Uncle, then I'll tell you something else. The girl is now eight years old and still living in a state of ignorance because you won't let her be educated. They told me in the village you wouldn't let her go to school or to church – my only sister's daughter. I'm responsible for her welfare, and when a child has an opportunity in her grasp such as Heidi has now only a person who doesn't care a fig for anyone's well-being could stand in her way. But I won't give in, I can tell you, and I've got everyone on my side. There's nobody in the village that won't help me against you. And if it ever comes to court, Uncle, then just remember there are things that could be raked up about you that you'd rather not hear, because once a court case gets underway all sorts of half-forgotten stories are given an airing."

"Hold your tongue!" bellowed the Alp Uncle, his eyes ablaze. "Take her and ruin her! But never let me have sight of her again. I don't want to see her with a feather in her hat spouting words like yours today!" And he strode out of the door.

CHAPTER 5

"You've made Grandfather angry," said Heidi, and the flash-ing black eyes she fixed on her aunt were far from friendly.

"He'll get over it. Now come on," Dete urged her. "Where are your clothes?"

"I'm not coming," said Heidi.

"What was that?" her aunt snapped, before modulating to a half-friendly, half-cross tone. "Come, come, you don't properly understand, but you're going to have it better than you could ever imagine." Then she went over to the cupboard, took out Heidi's things and made them into a bundle. "So come on, pick up your hat. It doesn't look too good, but it will do for now. Put it on and let's be gone!"

"I'm not coming," Heidi repeated.

"You're being as silly and stubborn as a goat. Have you learnt it from them? Listen to me now. You saw Grandfather was angry. He said he didn't wish to see us again, which means he wants you to come with me, so you mustn't make him even angrier by disobeying. You have no idea how lovely it is in Frankfurt. There's so much to see, and if you don't like it you can come back home. By that time Grandfather will have calmed down."

"Could I turn round on the spot and come home this evening?" Heidi asked.

"Honestly! Come along now. As I say, you can return whenever you like. Today we go as far as Maienfeld, and early tomorrow we'll be on the train. And the train can bring you back again in an instant – as quick as flying."

As she spoke, Dete slipped the bundle of clothes under her arm and took Heidi's hand. Together they set off down the mountain.

The pasture season had not yet begun, and Peter was still going to school in the village. Or he should have been, but now and again he had a day off, reckoning it a waste of time since learning to read was not really necessary, and instead he ambled about in search of big switches, which were of practical use. On this particular day he was nearing his home, bearing evidence of his fruitful endeavours on his shoulder in the form of a great sheaf of long, thick hazel switches. When he spotted the two approaching figures he stood still and stared until they reached him.

"Heidi, where are you going?" he asked.

"I just have to go to Frankfurt quickly with Aunt Dete," she answered. "But first I'll go in and see Grandmother. She'll be expecting me."

"No, absolutely not, we're running late as it is," said her aunt hurriedly, keeping tight hold of Heidi's hand as she tried to break away. "You can visit her when you get home again. Come on now!"

And she pulled Heidi firmly onwards, fearing that if she released her to go into the cottage she might set her mind against the journey, and that Peter's grandmother might well take her side.

Meanwhile Peter burst into the cottage and – needing to vent his feelings – crashed his whole sheaf of switches against the table so hard that everything in the room rattled. Grandmother gave a plaintive shriek and jumped up from her spinning wheel.

"What's the matter? What's the matter?" cried the frightened old woman, while his mother, who had been sitting at the table and had almost flown into the air when the sheaf struck it, spoke in her usual long-suffering tone: "What is it, Peter dear? Why are you being so wild?"

"Because she's taken Heidi," Peter replied.

"Who has, Peter, who? And taken her where?" asked Grandmother with growing alarm. But she quickly guessed what had occurred, her daughter having told her not long before that she had seen Dete going up towards the Alp Uncle's cottage. Trembling with haste, Grandmother got the window open and called out imploringly: "Dete, Dete, don't take the child away from us. Don't take Heidi away!"

The two receding figures could just hear her voice, and Dete must have guessed her meaning, for she increased her grip on Heidi's hand and walked as fast as she could. Heidi tried to resist. "That was Grandmother calling," she said. "I want to go to her."

This was the last thing her aunt wanted, so she pacified the girl and told her they should hurry up to avoid being late. That way they could travel on to Frankfurt the next day, Dete said, and she would soon see that she liked it far too much there ever to wish to leave again. But if she did prefer to come home she could do so straight away and bring something for Grandmother that would give her pleasure. This prospect appealed to Heidi, and she ceased to resist their forward rush.

"What could I bring for Grandmother?" she asked after a few moments.

"Something nice," answered Dete. "Some lovely soft, white rolls – she'd love them. She finds the brown ones almost impossible to eat now."

"Yes," Heidi agreed, "she always gives them to Peter and says they're too hard for her. I've seen that myself. Let's go quickly then, Aunt Dete, and maybe we'll make it to Frankfurt today and I can soon be back with the rolls."

Heidi began to run, and her aunt, with the bundle under her arm, could scarcely keep up. But she was very glad their progress was so rapid, for they had now reached the first houses of the village, where they might have faced all sorts of comments and enquiries that could have changed Heidi's mind again. Dete made a beeline through the village, with Heidi pulling so hard at her hand that everyone could see it was the girl who was setting their pace. To all the questions shouted from doorways and windows Dete replied: "I can't stop now, as you see. The child is in a hurry, and we have a long way to go."

"Are you taking her with you?" – "Is she running away from the Alp Uncle?" – "It's a wonder she's still alive!" – "But what red cheeks she has!" Such were the exclamations coming from all sides, and Dete was thankful that she was not held up and made to give a proper explanation, and that Heidi also said nothing, but pressed on with great urgency.

From that day onwards the Alp Uncle was more grim-faced than ever when he came down and passed through the village. He greeted no one, and with his sack of cheeses on his back, his outsized stick in his hand and his thick eyebrows knitted together he looked so menacing that mothers would say to their little ones, "Watch out! Keep out of the Alp Uncle's path or he might harm you!"

The old man ignored them all as he made his way deep into the valley, where he sold his cheeses and bought provisions of bread and meat. The villagers would stand about in little groups behind him after he had gone by, everyone volunteering some new observation about him – that he looked wilder than before, and that he no longer even acknowledged the greetings of others. They all agreed it was a mercy that the child had escaped from his clutches. Had they not seen her eagerness to get away, as if she feared he would come after her and fetch her back?

Only Peter's blind grandmother stayed loyal to the Alp Uncle, and she told anyone who came to see her with yarn to spin or spun yarn to collect how kind and thoughtful he had been towards Heidi. She also spoke of the good turn he had done her and her daughter by spending many afternoons patching up their house, which but for his help would certainly have fallen down. Reports of her statements circulated in the village, but most people who heard them said she was probably too old to know what was going on and had most likely misunderstood something. Since she was blind there was every chance she was rather deaf as well.

The Alp Uncle was no longer seen at the goatherd's cottage, and it was a good thing he had repaired it so well, for no one else touched it for a long time. Grandmother's days once more began with a sigh, and none ever elapsed without the same lamentation passing her lips: "Ah, with the child all the joy and light has gone out of our lives, and the days are so empty now! If I could hear Heidi just one more time before I die!"

Chapter 6

A Whole New World

A T THE HOME OF HERR SESEMANN in Frankfurt his sickly daughter Klara was sitting in the comfortable wheelchair in which she spent her days and could be pushed from room to room. At present she was in the so-called schoolroom, just off the large dining room, amid the clutter of objects and implements that made for a homely look and showed the room to be in constant use. A big, handsome glass-fronted bookcase justified the room's name, suggesting that it was here the lame girl received her daily lessons.

Klara had mild blue eyes peering out of a pale, narrow face. Just now these eyes were directed at the large wall clock, which seemed to go particularly slowly today, and, in a testy voice at odds with her usually patient nature, she said, "Is it still not time, Fräulein Rottenmeier?"

The woman to whom this question was addressed was sitting very upright at a small work table with her embroidery. She was mysteriously concealed under a cloak with a capelet and large collar, and the solemn appearance this gave her was accentuated by the tall, dome-like structure of hair on her head. Fräulein Rottenmeier had entered Herr Sesemann's house several years earlier, following the death of his wife. She ran the household and supervised all the servants. Herr Sesemann was mostly away on business, and he entrusted her with the entire running of his home on the condition that his daughter have a say in everything and nothing be done against her wishes.

At the same moment that Klara upstairs fretfully enquired of Fräulein Rottenmeier for a second time whether those they were expecting would soon arrive, Dete stood by the front door holding Heidi's hand and asked the coachman Johann, who had just descended from his box, if it was too late to disturb Fräulein Rottenmeier.

"I wouldn't know," the coachman growled. "Ring for Sebastian when you get into the corridor."

Dete did so, and the manservant came down the stairs. He had large, round buttons on his livery and almost equally large, round eyes in his head.

"I wanted to know if it's too late to disturb Fräulein Rottenmeier," Dete again enquired.

"I wouldn't know," replied Sebastian. "Ring the other bell for Tinette, the maid." And without troubling himself further he disappeared.

Another ring from Dete brought Tinette to the top of the stairs, with a small, brilliant white cap placed squarely on her head and a scornful expression on her face. "What is it?" she asked, without descending. Dete repeated her request. Tinette made off, but soon reappeared and shouted down, "They're expecting you."

Dete and Heidi went up the stairs and followed the maid into the schoolroom. Dete stood politely just inside the door and, having no idea how Heidi might behave in such unfamiliar surroundings, kept a firm hold of her hand.

Fräulein Rottenmeier slowly rose from her chair and crossed the room to take a look at the newly arrived companion for the daughter of the house. She did not appear quite pleased with what she saw. Heidi was in her plain woollen dress and had her old, crumpled straw hat on her head. She peered out innocuously from under its brim and stared with undisguised amazement at the edifice on top of the lady's head.

"What is your name?" asked Fräulein Rottenmeier after a few moments scrutinizing the child, who likewise did not take her eyes off her.

"Heidi," she replied in a clear, bell-like voice.

"What? No Christian has ever been called that. I can't believe you were baptized with that name. What name were you given in baptism?"

"I don't remember."

"What an answer!" said the housekeeper, shaking her head. "Dete, is the child simple or is she being saucy?"

"Begging your pardon, Madam, but if you please I'm happy to speak for her as she's unused to strangers," Dete replied, having given Heidi a surreptitious prod for her unseemly answer. "She isn't simple and nor is she saucy

– she wouldn't know how. She just says what comes into her head. This is her first time in a gentleman's house and her manners want polish, but if you kindly bear with her you will find her docile and well disposed. She was baptized Adelheid after her mother, my late sister."

"That's more like it, a name I can pronounce," remarked Fräulein Rottenmeier. "But Dete, I must say she seems curiously young. I told you Miss Klara's companion was to be of her own age, so that she could follow the same lessons and share her other occupations. Miss Klara has already turned twelve. How old is this child?"

Dete's answer was fluent: "If you please, Madam, the truth is I wasn't quite sure of her age. She is indeed a little younger than Miss Klara, but not a great deal. I couldn't say exactly, but I would guess she's probably about ten, if not more."

"I'm eight now. I know that from Grandfather," Heidi put in. Her aunt prodded her a second time, but Heidi had no idea why and showed no embarrassment.

"What? Only eight years old?" Fräulein Rottenmeier was indignant. "Four years too young! How is that supposed to work? And what about your education? What books have you been taught with?"

"None," said Heidi.

"What, none? How have you learnt to read, then?"

"I haven't, and nor has Peter."

"Mercy me! You can't read. Really can't read!" cried Fräulein Rottenmeier, horror-stricken. "How is it possible that you can't read? Well, what have you been taught?"

"Nothing," replied Heidi truthfully.

For a few moments Fräulein Rottenmeier struggled to keep her countenance. "Dete," she said finally, "this isn't at all what we agreed. How could you bring me a child like this?"

But Dete was not so easily browbeaten, and she answered warmly: "If you please, Madam, I thought she was exactly what you wanted. You described what you were looking for, something a bit different and not just the ordinary sort of girl. I had to pick this one, because the older ones back home don't have that quality any more, and I thought she would suit you perfectly. I must go now, because my mistress is expecting me back. If she lets me, I'll come again soon and see how the girl is getting on." With a curtsy she was out of the door and down the stairs in double-quick time.

For a moment Fräulein Rottenmeier did not move. Then she ran after Dete, realizing there were all sorts of things she still needed to discuss with her if the child really was to stay, though clearly she was already on their hands and Dete determined to leave her there.

Heidi still stood on the spot near the door that she had occupied since entering the room. Klara, who had observed the preceding scene in silence from her wheelchair, now beckoned to her and said, "Come here." Heidi went up to her.

"Would you rather be called Heidi or Adelheid?" Klara asked.

"I'm called Heidi and nothing else," came the answer.

"Then that's what I'll always call you," said Klara. "I think it suits you. I haven't heard it before, but then I

76

haven't seen a girl like you before. Have you always had your hair so short and curly?"

"Yes, I think so."

"Are you glad to be in Frankfurt?"

"No, but tomorrow I'm going home again with some white rolls for Grandmother!" Heidi replied.

"What a strange girl you are!" exclaimed Klara. "You've been brought to Frankfurt specially to be with me and join me in my lessons. And you know, it will be great fun because you can't read, and that's something new that will make the lessons different. Otherwise they can be so terribly dull that the mornings never seem to end. Because, you see, the lessons start every morning at ten o'clock when the tutor arrives and go on till two – it's such a long time. Sometimes the tutor holds his book right up to his face as if he had suddenly become short-sighted, but it's only to hide his enormous yawns. It's the same with Fräulein Rottenmeier: she takes out her big handkerchief now and again and covers her face as though she were moved by what we're reading, but I know perfectly well she's just yawning like mad behind it. And then I'd like a good yawn too, but I have to stop myself because if I ever let out a single one Fräulein Rottenmeier would say I was off-colour and fetch the cod liver oil, and cod liver oil is such awful stuff that I'd rather stifle my yawns. But now I'll be able to listen while you learn to read, and that will be much more interesting."

Heidi shook her head dubiously at the notion of learning to read.

"Yes, Heidi, of course you must learn to read. Everyone must, and the tutor's a very nice man. He explains everything and never gets angry. But you know, when he explains something you won't understand any of it. Then you just have to wait and say nothing, otherwise he'll explain even more and you'll understand even less. But afterwards, when you've taken it in and understood it, you'll realize what he was trying to say."

At this point Fräulein Rottenmeier re-entered the room, visibly flustered at not having succeeded in calling Dete back, for she had much more to say about how far the child was from meeting her requirements. Her uncertainty about what she should do to reverse the step she had taken made her all the more agitated, especially as the whole scheme had been her idea. She hurried into the dining room, back into the schoolroom and into the dining room again before letting fly at Sebastian, who at that moment was casting his round eyes thoughtfully over the freshly laid table to see if anything was wrong with his handiwork.

"Maybe if you put off your daydreaming till tomorrow we'll have a chance of dinner this evening."

After delivering herself of these words, Fräulein Rottenmeier stalked past Sebastian and called out for Tinette so peremptorily that the maid made her short mincing steps shorter still as she approached. When she appeared, her face wore such a sardonic look that even Fräulein Rottenmeier dared not tick her off, which only increased her inner turmoil.

"See that the new girl's room is made up, Tinette," she said, struggling to maintain her composure. "Everything is ready for you, and don't forget to dust the furniture."

"Nothing could be too much trouble," scoffed the maid as she walked away.

Meanwhile, Sebastian, not brave enough to vent his fury by answering Fräulein Rottenmeier back, instead thrust open the double doors from the dining room with a bang. Then he stepped nonchalantly into the schoolroom to take Klara through in her wheelchair. As he was adjusting one of the chair's handles that had twisted itself round, Heidi planted herself in front of him and looked at him intently. On noticing her Sebastian gave a start. "What do you think you're staring at?" he asked with a growl, which he would not have done if he had noticed Fräulein Rottenmeier coming back into the room. She crossed the threshold just as Heidi made her reply: "You look just like Peter the Goatherd."

The housekeeper clasped her hands in dismay. "Is it really possible!" she groaned in a low voice. "Now she's being familiar with the servants! The creature has no notion how to behave."

Sebastian wheeled Klara into the dining room and then lifted her onto a seat at the table. Fräulein Rottenmeier sat on the same side and motioned to Heidi to take her place opposite. No one else joined them, and as they sat far apart at the large table Sebastian had plenty of room to serve the dishes. Beside Heidi's plate was a fine white roll, a sight that brought joy to her eyes. The resemblance to Peter that she had discovered in Sebastian must have made her feel that she could trust him implicitly. She sat as still and quiet as a mouse until he came up to her and presented her with a large dish of fried fish, and then she pointed to the roll and asked, "Can I keep this?" He nodded and shot a sideways glance at Fräulein Rottenmeier, curious to see what she would make of this question. Heidi instantly grabbed the roll and stuffed it in her pocket. Sebastian was hard put to keep a straight face, but he knew very well it was not his place to laugh. He remained standing next to Heidi, silent and motionless, because speaking and moving off were not permitted until she had helped herself. Heidi looked at him for a few moments in bemusement before asking, "Should I eat that as well?" Sebastian nodded. "Give me some, then," she said, looking calmly at her empty plate. Sebastian's features grew more contorted and the dish in his hands trembled perilously.

"You may put the dishes on the table and return for them later," said Fräulein Rottenmeier with a stern look. Sebastian left the room at once.

"As for you, Adelheid," she continued with a deep sigh, "I can see I'll have to teach you even the most basic things, first and foremost how to help yourself at table." And she demonstrated in careful detail everything Heidi had to do. "Furthermore, I must impress on you that you are not to speak to Sebastian while we dine, and otherwise only when you have instructions for him or need to ask him a question. And you must never be familiar with him. Is that clear? I hope never again to hear the like of what you said to him just now. And the same goes for Tinette. You will address me as Fräulein Rottenmeier, as everyone does, and what you are to call Klara she can decide for herself."

"Klara, of course," said Klara.

Fräulein Rottenmeier followed these remarks with a host of directions about general conduct: getting up and going to bed, entering and leaving rooms, tidying up after one-self, shutting doors. As she spoke Heidi's eyes gradually closed, for she had risen before five o'clock that morning and made a long journey. She leant back in her chair and fell asleep. Some while later Fräulein Rottenmeier came to the end of her tutorial and asked, "Now, keep all that in mind, Adelheid! Have you understood everything I've said?"

"Heidi's been asleep for ages," said Klara, a big smile on her face. She had not had such an entertaining dinner for a long time.

"It's quite unheard of, what one has to endure with this child," exclaimed Fräulein Rottenmeier in a fury, and she rang the bell so violently that Tinette and Sebastian both came tumbling into the room. But Heidi slept on through the noise, and they had some trouble to rouse her sufficiently to take her through the schoolroom, Klara's bedroom and Fräulein Rottenmeier's sitting room to the corner bedroom that had been prepared for her.

Chapter 7

An Anxious Day for Fräulein Rottenmeier

WHEN HEIDI AWOKE on her first morning in Frankfurt, she could not believe her eyes. She gave them a good rub and looked again, but what she saw did not change. She was in a high white bed, and before her was a large, square room with white curtains of great length that screened the daylight. The room contained two chairs stitched with big flowers near the window, a sofa of the same pattern against the wall with a round table in front of it, and in the corner a washstand bearing articles she had never previously seen. Suddenly she realized she was in Frankfurt and recalled the events of the previous day, particularly the instructions the lady had given her – at least those she had heard.

Heidi jumped down from her bed and dressed. Then, wanting to see the sky and the scenery outside, she went over to one window and then the other to draw back the big curtains, which gave her the feeling of being caged. But she could not shift them, and so instead she crept behind one pair to get to a window, which was so high that she could only just peer out over the sill. Heidi did not find what she was looking for. She ran to the second window and then back to the first, but all she saw from them were walls and windows, and then more walls and more windows.

She grew quite alarmed. It was still early morning, for Heidi's habit in the mountains was to get up early and rush out of the cottage to see how things looked, whether the sky was blue and the sun already up, whether the fir trees were swishing in the breeze and the little flowers had opened their throats. Like a bird placed for the first time in a glittering cage, which darts this way and that, investigating every perch to see where it might slip through and fly out to freedom, so Heidi kept running between the two windows and tried to get them open. Surely she would then see more than walls and windows, surely the bare earth and green grass below and the last patches of melting snow on the distant slopes would be visible. Longing for all this, she turned and pulled at the window handles and tried to squeeze her little fingers under the frames and use all her strength to raise them up, but nothing budged even a fraction and the windows stayed firmly shut. After a while, seeing that her exertions were in vain, Heidi gave up and began wondering whether she should instead go outside the house. She remembered from her arrival the day before that the area to the front was paved, but she would go round to the back to reach the open country.

Just then there was a knock at the door and Tinette poked her head inside. "Breakfast is served!" she said curtly.

Heidi had no idea what this meant, but Tinette's derisive features seemed to express a clear warning not to get too close to her rather than a friendly invitation, and Heidi interpreted her words accordingly. She therefore picked up a small stool from under the table, put it in a corner and sat down to await quietly whatever would happen next. A moment or two later she heard someone bustle towards her room. It was Fräulein Rottenmeier, who was once again in a flurry. "What's the matter with you, Adelheid?" she called into the room. "Don't you know what breakfast is? Now come along."

This Heidi understood, and she followed right away. Klara, who had been seated at the dining table for some time, gave her a friendly greeting. Her face was far more cheerful than usual, because she foresaw that this day too would bring all sorts of novelties. Breakfast passed without incident: Heidi ate her buttered bread decently, and then Klara was wheeled into the schoolroom. Fräulein Rottenmeier told Heidi to go in too and stay with Klara until the tutor came to begin the lessons.

Once the girls were alone, Heidi asked, "How can I look out of the house and see right down to the ground?"

"You have to open a window and lean forward," Klara answered with amusement.

"But the windows won't open," said Heidi sadly.

"Yes, they will," Klara assured her. "You can't do it, and I can't help you. But if you see Sebastian, ask him, and he'll open one for you."

It was quite a relief for Heidi to know that the windows opened and she could look out, because her room had made her feel shut in like a prisoner. Then Klara began asking her about her home life, and Heidi spoke with pleasure of the mountains, the goats and the pastureland, and of all the things she held dear.

When the tutor arrived, Fräulein Rottenmeier did not take him straight into the schoolroom as she generally did. First she had to unburden herself, and to this end she led him to the dining room, where they sat down and she gave him a breathless account of her predicament and how she had got into it.

A while back she had written to Herr Sesemann, then staying in Paris, that his daughter had long wished for a companion to live in the house with them, and that she herself felt that having another girl would be a spur to Klara in her lessons and stimulating company in her free time. Fräulein Rottenmeier had her own reasons for forwarding this plan, for she was keen to have someone who could relieve her of the task of keeping Klara amused when this was too much for her, which it frequently was. Herr Sesemann had replied that he would gladly fulfil his daughter's wish, but on the understanding that her companion should be treated as her equal in all things – he did not want an ill-used child in his house. "A quite needless observation on his part," Fräulein Rottenmeier added, "for who would want to ill-use children?"

She went on to tell the tutor how horribly she had been taken in and gave all the evidence of the child's staggering ignorance that she had seen so far. Just as his lessons would quite literally have to begin with the letters of the alphabet, so her more general instruction of the girl would have to start from first principles. She could see only one way out of this dilemma, and that was for him to declare that such dissimilar girls could not be taught together without serious detriment to the more advanced of the two. This would be a strong argument for ending the arrangement, and Herr Sesemann would concede the necessity of sending the new girl back home, but she could not take this step on her own authority now that he knew she had arrived. However, the tutor was a cautious man who never came to a decided view of anything. He offered some flowery words of comfort and suggested that if his new pupil lagged behind in some areas she might well be ahead in others, and that a well-regulated course of lessons would presently restore everything to its proper balance.

When Fräulein Rottenmeier saw that he intended to revert to teaching the alphabet rather than support her cause, she opened the door to the schoolroom for him and then quickly closed it again. She stayed on the other side because she could not bear the thought of going through the alphabet again. Then she paced up and down the dining room with long strides, considering how the servants should address Adelheid. Herr Sesemann had written that she was to be treated exactly like his daughter, and by this she imagined he was referring principally to relations with servants.

She had not pondered this question for long when she was disturbed by a frightful clatter of falling objects in the schoolroom followed by a cry for help to Sebastian. She dashed into the room to find everything in a heap on the floor: school implements, textbooks, exercise books, an ink bottle, all overspread by the tablecloth, from under which a stream of black ink flowed across the length of the room. Heidi had vanished.

"I might have known!" cried Fräulein Rottenmeier, wringing her hands. "Tablecloth, books, work basket, everything ruined! I've never seen anything like it. It's that wretched girl, no doubt."

The tutor stood dumbfounded and stared at the devastation. It was a terrible sight, and there could be only one cause. However, Klara was following this exceptional turn of events and its consequences with a broad smile. "Yes, Heidi did it," she explained, "but she didn't mean to, so she definitely shouldn't be punished. She was just in such a mad rush to get away that she pulled the tablecloth with her and everything fell to the floor. There were many carriages going by outside all at once – that's what made her shoot off. Maybe she hasn't seen one before."

Fräulein Rottenmeier turned on the tutor: "Do you see what I mean now? The girl doesn't have the first notion! Absolutely no idea what lessons even are, or that she's supposed to sit still and listen. But where has the little mischief-maker gone? Run away, perhaps! What would Herr Sesemann say?..."

She hurried out and down the stairs. By the open front door she found Heidi standing and gazing up and down the street with a bemused look on her face.

"What is it? What are you doing? How could you just run off like that?" Fräulein Rottenmeier scolded.

"I heard the fir trees rustling, but I don't know where they are and I can't hear them any more," Heidi replied, and she turned her head sadly to the side on which she had heard the rumbling of the carriages die away. To her ears this noise had sounded like the föhn wind rushing through the boughs, prompting her to run elatedly out of the house.

"Fir trees! Do you think we're in a forest? What wild fancies! Now come up and see the mess you've made!" With that Fräulein Rottenmeier went back upstairs. Heidi followed her and was astonished by the scene of utter havoc she found. In her joyful haste to reach the firs she had not noticed that she was dragging anything after her.

"Make sure you never do this again," said Fräulein Rottenmeier, pointing to the floor. "During lessons you are to sit still and pay attention. If you can't manage that by yourself, I'll have to bind you to the chair. Is that clear?"

"Yes," replied Heidi, "but I will sit still." She now understood that it was a rule not to move about during lessons.

Then Sebastian and Tinette had to come in to put the room to rights. The tutor went away, for there could be no further teaching until the next day, when the usual yawning could be resumed.

In the afternoons Klara always had to rest a while, and during that interval Heidi was to choose her own activity, as Fräulein Rottenmeier had informed her that morning. So when Klara reclined in her chair after lunch and Fräulein Rottenmeier retired to her room, Heidi knew the time for her own activity had come. This was very welcome to her as there was something she wanted to do. She needed help, though, and she stood in the middle of the corridor outside the dining room so as not to miss the person she intended to ask. Sure enough, after a few moments Sebastian came up the stairs carrying a tea tray loaded with silverware from the kitchen to be put away in the dining-room cupboard. When he reached the top Heidi went up to him and said loud and clear: "Mr Sebastian!"

Sebastian opened his eyes as wide as physically possible and said rather gruffly: "What you mean by that, miss?"

"I'd just like to ask you something, but it's definitely nothing bad like this morning." Heidi said this in a conciliatory tone, having sensed that he was rather vexed and putting it down to the spillage of ink.

"Right, but first I'd like to know why you're calling me Mr Sebastian," he retorted in the same gruff tone.

"I'm not allowed to be familiar," Heidi explained. "Fräulein Rottenmeier said so."

At once Sebastian realized what the housekeeper must have told her, and he roared with laughter. Heidi looked at him in bafflement, for she was unaware of having said anything funny. Amid his mirth Sebastian now said, "Very good, miss. Please continue."

Now it was Heidi's turn to be put out: "My name isn't 'miss'. It's Heidi."

"That's all very well, but the very same lady has ordered me to say 'miss'," he informed her.

"Has she? I'll have to accept it, then," said Heidi resignedly. She had seen that Fräulein Rottenmeier's orders always had to be obeyed. "Now I've got three names," she added with a sigh.

"And what was your question, little miss?" enquired Sebastian, who had moved into the dining room and was putting the silver away in the cupboard.

"How do you open a window, Sebastian?"

He threw open a large casement. "Just like that!"

Heidi stepped up to it but was too small to see out, the top of her head just about reaching the sill.

Sebastian brought over a high wooden stool and placed it in front of her: "Here, miss, now you can look out and see down to the ground."

Heidi climbed on the stool, delighted that she would at last be able to put her head out of the window as she wished. A second later she pulled it back in again with a look of deep disappointment. "The only thing I can see here is the paved street – nothing else at all," she said sorrowfully. "But, Sebastian, if I go round to the other side of the house what will I see there?"

"Exactly the same," he replied.

"So where should I go to see right across the whole valley?"

"You'd have to climb a tall tower, a church tower, like the one over there with the golden dome on top. From there you can look down and see everything far into the distance."

Heidi quickly got off the stool and ran to the door, down the stairs and out into the street. But what she had in mind proved more difficult than she had imagined. Looking from the window, it had seemed that she only needed to cross the street to stand in front of the tower. But now she walked to the end of the street without reaching it and without even being able to see it any more. She turned into another street and went farther and farther, but still no tower. A great many people passed her, but all in such a hurry that Heidi thought they would not have time to stop and tell her the way. At the next corner she saw a boy standing with a small barrel organ on his back and an odd-looking animal on his arm. Heidi hastened towards him and asked, "Where's the tower with the golden dome?"

"Don't know," came the answer.

"Who can I ask about it?"

"Don't know."

"Do you know another church with a tall tower?" Heidi pressed on.

"Yes, I know one."

"So come and show me."

"What will you give me if I do?" The boy held out his hand.

Heidi rummaged in her pocket and pulled out a pretty little painting of a garland of red roses. She considered it for a moment or two with regret, because it had been a present from Klara that very morning. But oh, to look down past the green slopes into the valley! "Here," she said, proffering the picture. "Do you want this?"

The boy withdrew his hand and shook his head.

"What, then?" asked Heidi, glad to put the picture back in her pocket.

"Money."

"I haven't got any, but Klara has. She'll give me some. How much do you want?"

"Twenty pfennigs."

"Well, come on then."

Together they wandered down a long street. On the way Heidi asked her companion what he was carrying on his back, to which he replied that under the cloth was a fine organ that played beautiful music when he turned the handle. Suddenly they came to an old church with a tall tower. The boy halted and said, "There it is!"

"But how can I get in?" asked Heidi, who saw that the doors were shut fast.

"Don't know."

"Do you think I could ring, like they do for Sebastian?"

"Don't know."

Heidi had discovered a bell on the wall, and she now pulled it with all her might. "Wait here if I go up, because I don't know the way back and you'll have to show me."

"What will you give me?"

"What do you want?"

"Another twenty pfennigs."

Just then the old lock was turned from inside and the door opened with a creak. An elderly man emerged and looked first in surprise, then in some annoyance, at the children. "What are you playing at, fetching me down like this?" he berated them. "Can't you read what it says over the bell? 'Ring if you wish to ascend the tower.'"

Rather than answering, the boy pointed his finger at Heidi. She said, "That's just what I want to do."

"What for?" asked the tower warden. "Has someone sent you?"

"No," Heidi replied, "I'd just like to go up so I can see down."

"Be off with you now, and don't pull that stunt again, because I won't let you off so easily a second time!" With that the warden turned about and made to close the door.

But Heidi held on to his coat-tails. "Just this once!" she pleaded.

He looked round, and Heidi's upturned eyes were so imploring that he was quite won over. He took her by the hand and said kindly, "If it means so much to you, then come on!"

The boy sat down on a stone step by the door to indicate that he was staying behind. Inside Heidi went up a long, long stairway, her hand in the warden's. Gradually the steps narrowed and the walls closed in, until at last they reached the top. The warden lifted the child up to let her see out of the open window.

"There now, look down," he said.

Heidi's eyes were met with a sea of roofs, towers and chimneys. Soon she drew in her head and said in a small voice, "That's not what I expected at all."

"Just as I thought. What can a young thing like you know about views? So let's go down again and don't go ringing outside any more churches!"

He set her on the floor again and led the way down the narrow steps. On the left where they first widened was a door that opened into the warden's parlour, and next to it the floor ran under the sloping roof to form a recess. Here, well back, was a large basket, and a chunky grey cat sat and snarled in front of it. Her offspring lived in the basket, and she always warned passers-by against meddling in her family affairs. Heidi, who had never seen such a huge cat, stood and stared in amazement. The tower housed hordes of mice, so the cat was sure to catch half a dozen rodent delicacies each day without even trying. The old man noticed Heidi's surprise and said, "Come on, she won't harm you if I'm here, so you can take a look at the kittens."

She went up to the basket and broke out in whoops of delight. "Oh, the lovely little things! Such pretty kittens!" she said over and over, and she hopped from one side of the basket to the other to observe the comic pantomime performed by the seven or eight kittens as they scrambled, gambolled and tumbled tirelessly over one another.

"Do you want one to keep?" asked the warden, gladdened by the sight of the girl skipping with pleasure.

"What, just for me? For good?" gasped Heidi, scarcely able to believe her luck.

"Yes, of course. You can have more than one. The whole lot, if you've got room for them," said the man, glad to think he might get rid of the kittens without having to destroy them himself.

Heidi was beside herself with happiness. There was plenty of room in the large house, and how surprised and delighted Klara would be when she laid eyes on the sweet little creatures!

"But how can I carry them?" asked Heidi, attempting to catch a couple and then flinching back when their mother flew at her arm and hissed fiercely.

"I'll bring them to you if you tell me where," said the warden, stroking the cat soothingly. She was an old friend and had lived with him in the tower for many years.

"Herr Sesemann's, the big house where the front door has a golden dog's head with a thick ring through its snout," Heidi told him.

The warden did not need so much detail. He had occupied his perch in the tower for long enough to be familiar with every house far and wide. Moreover, Sebastian was an old acquaintance of his.

"I know it all right," he remarked. "But who should I ask for when I bring them? I'll have to give a name, and you're not a member of the family, are you?"

"No, but Klara is, and she'll be so thrilled when the kittens arrive."

The warden wanted to go on down, but Heidi could not tear herself away from the entertaining spectacle.

"If I could just take a couple now! One for me and one for Klara. Could I?"

"Wait a second," he replied. Carefully he carried the cat into his parlour and placed her in front of her food bowl, then came back out and closed the door behind him. "Right, take two now."

Heidi's eyes gleamed with joy. She lifted up a white kitten and one with white and ginger stripes, slipped them into her left and right pockets and went down the stairway with the warden. The boy was still sitting on the step outside. Once the warden had let Heidi out and shut the door she said, "How do we get from here to Herr Sesemann's house?"

"Don't know," came the answer.

Heidi began to describe what she knew of the house – its windows, its front door, its porch steps – but it meant nothing to the boy, who shook his head.

Then she thought of something else: "Listen, from one window you can see a great big grey house, and the roof goes like this," and she sketched a zigzag in the air with her forefinger.

Now the boy leapt up. It was features like this that he used to find his way around. He set off at pace with Heidi on his heels, and in no time they arrived at the front door with its large brass dog's head. Heidi rang the bell, and soon Sebastian appeared. When he saw her he urged her inside: "Quick! Quick!"

She darted into the house and Sebastian closed the door, not even noticing the bewildered boy standing next to her.

"Quick, miss, straight into the dining room," Sebastian pressed. "They're already sitting at table, and Fräulein Rottenmeier looks like a powder keg. What possessed you to run away like that?"

The housekeeper did not raise her eyes when Heidi entered the room. Klara said nothing either, and there was an uneasy silence as Heidi sat down and Sebastian pushed her chair up to the table. Once this was done, Fräulein Rottenmeier looked at her sternly and began speaking in a solemn, formal tone: "We shall have words later, Adelheid, but for now I'll just say this: you have conducted yourself very badly and deserve to be punished. To leave the house without asking permission or saying a word to anyone and then roam around until well into the evening – it's absolutely outrageous."

"Meow" was all she received by way of a reply.

"What was that, Adelheid?" Fräulein Rottenmeier became irate, and her voice grew shrill. "How dare you make silly jokes after all your other bad behaviour! You'd better watch out, I can tell you!"

"I'm not..." Heidi began. "Meow! Meow!"

Sebastian all but threw the dishes on the table and lurched out of the room.

"Right, that will do," Fräulein Rottenmeier wanted to say, but her voice was choked with fury. "Get up and leave the room."

Heidi stood up in alarm and tried again to explain: "I'm really not..."

"Meow! Meow!"

"But Heidi," Klara put in, "why do you keep meowing when you can see how it upsets Fräulein Rottenmeier?"

"I'm not. The kittens are." At last Heidi explained herself without interruption.

"What was that? Kittens? Cats?" the lady shrieked. "Sebastian! Tinette! Find the horrid things and get them out of here!" And she shot into the schoolroom to save herself and bolted its doors, for nothing in all creation was so frightful to her as kittens.

Sebastian stood outside the dining room trying to recover from a fit of laughter before going in again. While serving Heidi he had spotted a kitten's head peeping out of her pocket and looked forward to a rumpus, and when it had broken out he could not contain himself and was barely able to set the dishes on the table. Now at last he regained his composure and went back in. By this time Fräulein Rottenmeier's cries of despair had fallen silent, and the scene that met his eyes was calm and peaceful. Klara had the kittens in her lap and Heidi was kneeling beside her, both girls blissfully happy as they played with the graceful little creatures.

"Sebastian," said Klara, "you have to help us find a nook for the kittens where Fräulein Rottenmeier won't see them, because they scare her and she wants to get rid of them. But we want to keep the sweet little things and fetch them out when we're alone. Where can we put them?"

"I'll see to that, Miss Klara," Sebastian answered readily. "I'll make a nice cosy bed for them in a basket and put it where the jittery lady won't find it. You can count on me." Sebastian set straight to work and sniggered continually under his breath. "There'll be a row about this all right!" he thought, and he was not averse to the idea of the housekeeper getting into a flap.

Not until much later, when bedtime was approaching, did Fräulein Rottenmeier open the door a crack and shout through it, "Have those dreadful animals been removed?"

"They have indeed!" answered Sebastian, who was keeping himself busy in the dining room in expectation of this question. Nimbly he swept the kittens up from Klara's lap and carried them off.

Fräulein Rottenmeier decided to postpone the sermon she intended for Heidi until the next day. For now she was too exhausted by the sequence of emotions – vexation, anger and fright – that the girl had quite unwittingly put her through. She retired without a word, and Klara and Heidi did the same, content in the knowledge that their kittens were comfortably settled.

Chapter 8

Troubled Times in Herr Sesemann's House

O N THE FOLLOWING MORNING Sebastian, having
opened the front door to the tutor and taken him
up to the schoolroom, heard someone else ringing the
bell outside so forcefully that he was back downstairs in
a shot. "Only Herr Sesemann himself rings like that," he
thought, "so he must have come home without warning."
He flung open the door and saw, standing before him, a
ragged boy with a barrel organ on his back.

"What do you think you're doing?" he barked. "I'll teach
you to pull bell cords like that! What do you want here?"

"I want to see Klara," the boy replied.

"You dirty street urchin, can't you say 'Miss Klara' like
we all do? What's your business with her anyway?" asked
Sebastian harshly.

"She owes me forty pfennigs," explained the boy.

"You must be a bit soft in the head! How do you even know Miss Klara lives here?"

"Yesterday I showed her the way somewhere – makes twenty pfennigs. Then I showed her the way back – makes another twenty!"

"See what great big fibs you're telling! Miss Klara never goes out. She can't walk. So clear off back where you belong or I'll clip you round the ear!"

But the boy refused to be intimidated. He stood his ground and said coolly, "But I saw her in the street and I can describe her. She had short, curly hair, black it was, and black eyes too. Her dress was brown, and she didn't talk like we do."

"Aha," thought Sebastian, chuckling inwardly, "that'll be the other little miss who's been up to more mischief."

He pulled the boy inside and said, "Fair enough. Follow me and wait outside the door till I come out again. Then, when I let you in, you can play a tune. Miss Klara will like that."

Upstairs, Sebastian knocked at the schoolroom door and was admitted. "There's a boy here who has something important to ask Miss Klara," he announced.

Klara was delighted at such an unusual circumstance. "Show him straight in," she said. And, turning to the tutor: "I hope you agree, sir. He needs to see me, it seems."

The boy was already in the room, and as instructed he immediately started to play his organ. Fräulein Rottenmeier was in the dining room, where she had found various things to do that would keep her from having to listen to the alphabet being taught. All at once she pricked up her ears. Were those sounds coming from the street? They seemed so near. Surely there couldn't be a barrel organ in the schoolroom. And yet… it really did seem… She strode all through the long dining room and tore open the door. There, before her unbelieving eyes, in the middle of the schoolroom, stood a scruffy organ-grinder turning his instrument with great zeal. The tutor was clearly trying to say something, but could not make himself heard. Klara and Heidi were listening to the music with beaming faces.

"Stop! Stop it immediately!" cried Fräulein Rottenmeier from the doorway. Her voice was drowned out by the music. She made to rush at the boy, but came to an abrupt halt when she sensed something on the floor beneath her. She looked down, and saw a ghastly, dark-coloured animal crawling between her feet – a tortoise. She leapt into the air, higher than she had done for many a year, and yelled at the top of her voice: "Sebastian! Sebastian!"

Suddenly the organ-grinder ceased his playing, for this time the voice had drowned out the music. Sebastian was standing on the other side of the half-open door, doubled up with laughter at the leap he had just witnessed. At last he came in. Fräulein Rottenmeier had collapsed into a chair.

"Away with them all, Sebastian, people and animals. Get them out of here this instant!" she commanded.

He willingly obeyed. He bundled the boy out of the house, only giving him time to pick up his tortoise, and then pressed something into his hand. "That's forty for Miss Klara and another forty for playing," he said. "That was well done!" With that he closed the front door on him.

In the schoolroom all was quiet again. Teaching had resumed, and this time Fräulein Rottenmeier had taken up her post there so she could prevent any further outrages in person. She intended to investigate what had happened after lessons were over and give the guilty party a punishment to remember. Presently there was another knock at the door and Sebastian again came in, this time with the news that a large basket had arrived for Miss Klara with orders that it be given to her directly.

"For me?" asked Klara, astonished and very curious to know more. "Bring it in at once, so I can see how it looks." Sebastian returned with a covered basket and then hurriedly left the room.

"We'd better finish lessons first and then unpack the basket," Fräulein Rottenmeier declared.

Klara could not imagine what the basket might contain and looked at it longingly. In the midst of declining a verb she broke off and said to the tutor, "Couldn't I just have a quick peep to see what's inside and then carry on?"

"There is something to be said both for and against the proposition," replied the tutor. "In its favour is the fact that, your attention having been diverted to this object…" He got no further with this speech. The basket's lid was loose, and suddenly one, two, three and then more little kittens hopped out from under it. With incredible speed they raced all round the room, giving the impression that their numbers had multiplied. They jumped over the tutor's boots and bit his trousers, clambered up Fräulein Rottenmeier's dress and crawled round her feet, sprang up onto Klara's chair and scrambled, scratched and meowed. It was a scene of utter confusion.

Klara was in raptures. "Oh, the adorable little things!" she exclaimed again and again. "Such funny gambols! Look at this one, Heidi, and that one over there!" Heidi too was all enjoyment, and she chased the kittens into every corner of the room. The tutor stood haplessly by his desk, lifting first one, then the other foot into the air to extricate them from the creepy scuttling on the floor.

At first Fräulein Rottenmeier sat speechless with terror in her chair, but then she began screaming with all her might: "Tinette! Tinette! Sebastian! Sebastian!" She dared not stand up in case the little horrors all jumped up at her.

Eventually Sebastian and Tinette appeared in response to her repeated cries for help, and Sebastian stuffed one after the other of the little creatures back in the basket, which he took up to the attic and placed alongside the bed he had made for the two kittens that had arrived the day before.

Thus a second day's lessons passed without any yawning. In the evening, by which time Fräulein Rottenmeier was sufficiently recovered from the morning's commotion, she summoned Sebastian and Tinette to the schoolroom in order to question them closely on the reprehensible incidents that had taken place. It then came out that Heidi had set them all in train during her escapade of the previous day. Fräulein Rottenmeier remained seated, white with indignation, and at first found no words to express her feelings. She waved Sebastian and Tinette out of the room and then turned to Heidi, who was standing next to Klara's wheelchair and did not quite comprehend what she had done wrong.

"Adelheid," she began severely, "I can only think of one punishment that you would be likely to feel. You're a little savage, but we shall see if a spell in the dark cellar, with its rats and lizards, won't tame you enough to stop such tricks from entering your head."

Heidi heard her sentence with quiet surprise, for she did not think of cellars as gruesome places. The adjoining room in Grandfather's cottage that he called the cellar, where newly made cheeses and fresh milk were stored, was a pleasant and inviting place. As for rats and lizards, she had never seen any.

But Klara raised her voice in distress: "No, no, Fräulein Rottenmeier, wait till Papa comes home! He has written to say he'll soon be here, and then I'll tell him everything and he'll decide what's to be done with Heidi."

Fräulein Rottenmeier could not dismiss this appeal to a higher authority, least of all as Herr Sesemann really was expected very soon. She stood up and said rather grimly, "As you wish, Klara, but I too will have a word with your father." With that she left the room.

A few days went by without incident, but Fräulein Rottenmeier was unable to shake off her agitation. Hourly she reflected on the way she had been duped about Heidi's character, and it seemed to her that since the girl had joined the Sesemann household everything had become topsy-turvy and could not be righted again.

Klara was in high spirits. She no longer felt bored during lessons because Heidi kept doing the most amusing things.

She always got her letters mixed up and could not remember them, and if the tutor explained them and described their shape to bring them home to her, perhaps mentioning a horn or a beak by means of comparison, she would interrupt him by gleefully blurting out "It's a goat!" or "It's an eagle!" His descriptions suggested all sorts of pictures to her mind, just not letters of the alphabet.

Later in the afternoons Heidi would sit with Klara and tell her at length about her life in the mountains, and the details she recalled made her so fiercely homesick that she always wound up with the words: "I really must go home now! Tomorrow I really will go!" But Klara always assuaged these feelings and made Heidi see that she could not possibly leave before her father's return, after which everything would be decided. Heidi always yielded and was soon content again, in part because she had a secret happy prospect: at lunch and dinner there was always a lovely white roll next to her plate, and these she pocketed, adding two more each day to the pile she was amassing for Grandmother. She could not have enjoyed eating them herself, because she knew that Grandmother never had any white rolls and was barely able to eat the hard brown ones.

After dinner each day Heidi would sit quite still and alone for a few hours in her room. She now understood that running out of doors, as she had done on the mountainside, was not permitted in Frankfurt, and she no longer did it. She could not go to the dining room for a chat with Sebastian, because Fräulein Rottenmeier would not permit that either, and the idea of starting a conversation with Tinette did not occur to her. The maid only ever spoke to her in a scornful manner and poked fun at her, and Heidi, who clearly understood that she was being mocked, always kept shyly out of her way. Thus she had all the time in the world to ponder how the pastureland would be green again and how the little yellow flowers would be sparkling in the sun, whose rays would illuminate the snow, the mountains and the whole valley.

At times the desire to be home again was unbearably strong, and had her aunt not told her she could go whenever she pleased? One day she could stand it no more. She hastily wrapped her bread rolls in the big red scarf, put on her straw hat and set off. But she got no farther than the front door when she encountered a great obstacle to her journey in the form of Fräulein Rottenmeier, who had been out and just returned. She came to a stop and looked Heidi up and down in a state of shock, staring particularly at the bulging red scarf.

Then she exclaimed, "What sort of costume is this? What's the meaning of it? Haven't I strictly forbidden you from wandering the streets any more? And now you're about to do it anyway, looking exactly like a vagrant to boot!"

"I wasn't going to wander the streets. I just wanted to go home," said Heidi, frightened.

"What? Go home? You wanted to go home?" Fräulein Rottenmeier frenziedly clapped her hands together. "You mean abscond! If ever Herr Sesemann finds out! Absconding from his house! You'd better make sure he doesn't hear of it. And what don't you like about living here? Aren't you far better treated than you deserve? Do you want for anything? Have you ever in your life had rooms or a dining table or service like you have here? Tell me!"

"No," Heidi replied.

"I should say not!" the housekeeper shot back. "You have everything you could wish for, you ungrateful wretch. In fact you have it so good that there's nothing for you to think of except what your next mischief will be."

At this all the feelings in Heidi's breast welled up and burst out of her: "I just want to go home, and if I stay away so long Snow Hop will always be bleating, and Grandmother is waiting for me, and Thistle Finch will be beaten if Peter the Goatherd doesn't get any cheese, and here you never see the sun saying goodnight to the mountains, and if the eagle ever flew over Frankfurt he would screech even louder, because there are so many people huddled together getting on each other's nerves instead of going higher up the slopes where they would feel better."

"Merciful Heavens, the child is out of her mind!" cried Fräulein Rottenmeier in horror. She dashed up the stairs, and at the top she hurtled straight into Sebastian, who was about to go down. "Go at once and bring that unfortunate creature up here," she snapped at him while rubbing her head, for it had been quite a collision.

"All right, and thank you kindly," he retorted while rubbing his own head, which had received an even bigger bang than hers.

Heidi had not moved. Her eyes were ablaze and her whole body shook with emotion.

"Well, what have you done this time?" asked Sebastian merrily. But when he had a better look at her and saw she did not stir he gave her a friendly pat on the shoulder and said comfortingly, "Now, now, you mustn't take it to heart, miss. Just keep smiling, that's the main thing! She nearly knocked a hole in my head, the way she ran into me. But don't let her break your spirit! What, still rooted to the spot? We'll have to go up, you know. She said so."

Heidi went upstairs, but slowly and silently, not at all like her usual self. Sebastian felt sorry to see her that way, and as he walked up behind her he spoke encouraging words: "Don't throw in the towel, just keep smiling and carry on regardless! What a sensible young miss you are – you haven't cried once since you came here! Most girls your age cry ten times a day, and that's a fact. And the kittens are happy in the attic, jumping about all over the place like little clowns. We'll go up together and have a look at them later when you-know-who isn't around."

Heidi gave a brief nod, but so listlessly that it pierced Sebastian's heart, and he watched her with real sympathy as she shuffled off to her room.

Fräulein Rottenmeier was tight-lipped at dinner that evening, but she kept glancing with a peculiar alertness towards Heidi, as if she half-expected her at any moment to do something bizarre. But Heidi, after quickly slipping a roll in her pocket, sat in silence, without moving a muscle, and she ate and drank nothing.

Next morning, as the tutor was mounting the stairs, Fräulein Rottenmeier mysteriously beckoned him into the dining room. There she informed him in a quavering voice of her worry that the change of air and lifestyle and new impressions had made the girl go to pieces. She told him of her attempted escape and repeated as many of her strange remarks as she could recall. But the tutor's response was calm and mollifying. He reassured her that while he had observed Adelheid to display signs of eccentricity, she nonetheless had a foundation of good sense, and that if handled with the judicious care he envisaged she would in time be restored to a proper equilibrium. To his mind her inability to grasp the alphabet despite his best endeavours constituted a weightier cause of concern.

Fräulein Rottenmeier felt easier after hearing this and released the tutor to his work. Towards the end of the afternoon, recollecting how Heidi had been attired for her planned departure, she decided to make her stock of clothes more respectable by adding various items of Klara's before Herr Sesemann came home. She spoke about this to Klara, who fully agreed and was happy to give Heidi any number of dresses, shawls and hats. So Fräulein Rottenmeier went into Heidi's room to look inside her wardrobe and determine what should be kept and what thrown away. Within a few minutes, however, she emerged looking quite disgusted.

"I can't believe what I've just seen, Adelheid!" she exclaimed. "I wouldn't have thought it possible! In your wardrobe, Adelheid, where you're supposed to keep clothes, right at the bottom, what do you think I found? A pile of bread rolls! Bread rolls, Klara, in the wardrobe! What an idea, to hoard them like that!" And she shouted across into the dining room, "Tinette, clear out all the old bread from Adelheid's wardrobe, and get rid of the crumpled straw hat on the table."

"No, no!" cried Heidi. "I need that hat, and the bread rolls are for Grandmother." She made to rush after Tinette, but Fräulein Rottenmeier caught hold of her.

"You stay here, and all that stuff will be taken where it belongs," she said sternly, still holding her back.

Then Heidi threw herself against Klara's chair and cried bitterly. She was in real despair, and her sobbing became loud and violent: "Now Grandmother won't have any bread rolls," she wailed again and again. "They were for her, and now they're all gone and she won't get any!" And she wept as if her heart would break.

Fräulein Rottenmeier ran from the room. Klara grew frightened by the sight of such wretchedness. "Heidi, Heidi, don't cry like that!" she pleaded. "Listen, don't get so upset! Look, I promise that when you go home I'll give you just as many rolls for your grandmother, or more, and they'll be fresh, soft ones, not hard like yours would be and probably are already. Come on Heidi, don't cry any more now!"

Heidi continued to cry for a while, and it was only because she understood Klara's consolation and took her at her word that she was able to stop at all. Several times, amid her final broken sobs, she asked Klara to confirm what she had said: "Will you give me just as many for Grandmother as I had before?"

And Klara kept reassuring her: "Yes, definitely, or even more. Cheer up now!"

Heidi's eyes were still red with crying when she appeared for dinner, and on seeing her bread roll she could not repress a few more tears. But, knowing she must be quiet at table, she soon took herself in hand. This evening Sebastian made the strangest gestures each time he came close to Heidi, pointing to his own head and then to hers, nodding repeatedly and screwing up his eyes, as if he wished to say "Don't worry! I know what's happened and I've sorted it out."

When Heidi went to her room afterwards and wanted to climb into bed she found her old straw hat concealed under the cover. Delighted, she pulled it out and lovingly pressed it into an even more crumpled shape. Then she covered it with a handkerchief and hid it in the farthest corner of the wardrobe.

It was Sebastian who had slipped it under her bedcover. He had been in the dining room with Tinette when she was summoned and he had heard her lamentation. So he followed Tinette, and when she stepped out of Heidi's room with an armful of rolls and the straw hat on top he snatched the hat and called back, "I'll dispose of this." He had rescued it very gladly, and his mute signals to Heidi during dinner were meant to raise her spirits by letting her know the hat was safe.

Chapter 9

Herr Sesemann Hears Many Strange Things

A FEW DAYS AFTER THESE EVENTS there was quite a commotion in the Sesemann household, with feet pounding up and down the stairs. The master had just returned from his journey and, piece by heavy piece, Sebastian and Tinette were carrying his luggage from the well-packed carriage to the first floor. Herr Sesemann always brought a heap of presents back from his trips. The first thing this gentleman did on arriving was to go and see his daughter in her room, where Heidi, as always at this time of the late afternoon, was sitting with her. Klara welcomed her father most fondly, for she loved him very much, and he was no less warm in greeting his beloved child. Then he extended his hand to Heidi, who had stolen into a corner, saying kindly, "And this is our little Swiss girl. Come, let me shake your hand! That's right. Now tell me, have you become good friends, you and Klara? Or do you squabble and get cross, and then cry and make up, and then go through the whole thing over again?"

"No, Klara is always nice to me," replied Heidi.

"And Heidi hasn't even thought of squabbling, Papa," put in Klara.

"Good, I'm glad to hear it," said her father, getting up from his chair. "And now, Klara, you'll have to excuse me while I go and eat something. I've had nothing all day. Then I'll come again and you'll see what I've brought home!"

As Herr Sesemann entered the dining room, Fräulein Rottenmeier was casting an eye over the table, which had been laid for him. Once he had taken his place and she had sat opposite him, looking a picture of misery, he turned to her and said, "Well, Fräulein Rottenmeier, what's the matter? You've received me today with a truly alarming countenance. What's wrong? Klara seems cheerful enough."

"Herr Sesemann," the housekeeper replied with the utmost gravity, "this affects Klara too. We have been most dreadfully let down."

"In what way?" he asked, calmly taking a sip of his wine.

"As you know, Herr Sesemann, we agreed to take a girl into the house as a companion for Klara and, mindful of your determination that she should only have good, true-hearted people about her, I turned my thoughts to a young Swiss girl. I hoped to find one like those I've often read about, born of the pure mountain air and wafting through life without their feet ever touching the ground."

"I rather suspect their feet do touch the ground," he countered. "Otherwise they wouldn't need any – they would need wings instead."

"Herr Sesemann, I think you know what I mean," she went on. "Such a being as one hears of, dwelling amid the lofty, unsullied peaks and floating by like a sublime essence."

"But Fräulein Rottenmeier, what earthly good would a sublime essence do for my Klara?"

"I'm not joking, Herr Sesemann. The situation is far graver than you suppose. I've been terribly – and I mean terribly – imposed upon."

"But what's so terrible? The child looks perfectly all right to me," said Herr Sesemann, unmoved.

"Well, just to mention one thing, Herr Sesemann: the people and animals she's filled your house with while you were away. The tutor can tell you all about that."

"Animals, Fräulein Rottenmeier? Please explain."

"There is no explanation, no way of accounting for the things the girl does unless one sees them as episodes of mental disturbance."

Up to this point Herr Sesemann had not been inclined to take the matter seriously. But mental disturbance? That really could have most regrettable consequences for his daughter. He stared hard at Fräulein Rottenmeier as if to assure himself it was not her mind that was unbalanced. Just then the door opened and the tutor was announced.

"Ah, here comes the tutor! He'll enlighten us, I'm sure. Do come in, my good fellow, and sit here beside me!" And he held out his hand to him. "We'll both have a cup of black coffee, please, Fräulein Rottenmeier. Do take a seat, young man, no need for ceremony. And now tell me, how are things with Klara's new companion, whom you are now teaching? What's all this about her bringing animals into the house, and would you say she is entirely rational?"

The tutor could not resist dwelling a little on his pleasure at Herr Sesemann's safe return and bidding him welcome – which indeed had been the reason for his visit – but when the other pressed him to answer his questions he did so in the following terms:

"If I had to express a view on the nature of this young girl, Herr Sesemann, I would wish first and foremost to emphasize that while on the one hand there is a backwardness in her development, caused by the marked neglect of her upbringing – or, to be more precise, by the somewhat delayed commencement of her education, together with her long sojourn in a secluded Alpine setting, albeit a setting that undoubtedly has certain merits and is not wholly to be condemned as long as its duration is not excessive, and which indeed may—"

"My dear fellow," Herr Sesemann interrupted, "please don't take such pains. Just tell me if the girl has shocked you by carting animals into the house, and what you think in general of her being with my daughter."

"I have no desire at all to speak ill of the girl," the tutor resumed, "for if, on the one hand, she displays an inexperience of society owing to the more or less uncultivated existence she led up to the time of her removal to Frankfurt – a removal which, in its consequences for the development of a girl who, in all or at least most regards, has fallen

behind but nonetheless has an appreciable natural apti-
tude, and who, if directed with careful attention to all—"

"Forgive me, please, I shouldn't have troubled you. I
shall… I really must go and look in on my daughter." And
Herr Sesemann hurried from the room, not to return. He
found the girls in the schoolroom, and Heidi stood up so
he could sit next to his daughter. Turning to Heidi, he said,
"Listen, poppet, could you run and… umm… run and
fetch me a…" and he racked his brains for something to
ask for, just to have her out of the room a few moments.
"Please fetch me a glass of water."

"Fresh water?"

"Yes please, as fresh as possible!"

Heidi disappeared.

"Now, my dear little Klara," he said, drawing his chair
closer to hers and laying her hand in his, "tell me in plain,
simple terms about the animals your playmate has brought
into the house and why Fräulein Rottenmeier thinks she's
sometimes not quite right in the head. Can you do that?"

She certainly could. The horrified woman had spoken
to her too about Heidi's bewildering speech, but to Klara
it made perfect sense. First she told her father all about
the tortoise and the kittens, then she explained Heidi's
comments that had so alarmed Fräulein Rottenmeier. Herr
Sesemann laughed heartily: "So, Klara, you don't want me
to send her home, then? You're not tired of her?"

"No, no, Papa, don't do that!" she said urgently. "Now
that Heidi's here things are always happening, every day,
and it's so much fun. Not like before, when nothing happened. And Heidi tells me so many stories."

"All right, Klara, don't worry. Ah, here comes your friend again. Well, did you find any nice fresh water?" he asked Heidi, as she handed him a glass.

"Yes, straight from the fountain," she replied.

"You didn't run to the fountain yourself, did you, Heidi?" asked Klara.

"Yes, of course, it's absolutely fresh. I had to go a long way, though. The first fountain had lots of people round it, so I went right down the street to the second one, but that was just the same. Then I turned into another street and got the water there, and the white-haired gentleman asked to be kindly remembered to Herr Sesemann."

"A successful expedition, then!" said Herr Sesemann with a laugh. "And who was the gentleman?"

"He was walking past the fountain, and he stopped and said, 'As you have a glass you could let me have a drink too. Who are you fetching water for?' He laughed out loud when I said 'Herr Sesemann', and he sent you his greeting and said he hoped you liked the water."

"Indeed! I wonder who my well-wisher was. How did he look?"

"He smiled in a friendly way and wore a thick gold chain that had something else golden with a big red stone hanging from it, and his stick had a horse's head on top."

"That's the doctor – that's the old doctor," said Klara and her father in unison, and Herr Sesemann chuckled inwardly at the thought of what his friend must have made of this novel way of getting in provisions of water.

Later that evening, as he sat alone with Fräulein Rottenmeier in the dining room talking over various household affairs, Herr Sesemann informed her that his daughter's companion was to remain with them. He considered her to be of sound mind, he said, and his daughter was fond of her and preferred her company to anyone else's. "I desire, therefore," he continued firmly, "that the girl should always be treated kindly and her peculiarities not be seen as misdemeanours. If you can't cope with her on your own, Fräulein Rottenmeier, you will find effective help at hand, for soon my mother will be coming for her usual long stay – and, as you well know, she can deal with any type of person."

"I do indeed know it, Herr Sesemann," she replied, but without any visible relief at the prospect of such assistance.

Herr Sesemann had only a short time to rest at home; after just two weeks he was obliged to travel to Paris on business. His daughter was unhappy that he was about to leave again, but he comforted her with the promise of her grandmother's arrival, which was expected in a few days.

Indeed, just after Herr Sesemann's departure a letter came from Frau Sesemann with the information that she was on the point of leaving Holstein, where she lived in an old manor house, and giving the expected time of her arrival the next day so that the carriage could be sent to meet her at the station.

Klara was overjoyed at this news, and that evening she spoke so much of her "Grandmamma" that Heidi began referring to her in the same way. This made Fräulein Rottenmeier frown, but Heidi, who felt constant disapproval from that quarter anyway, did not connect this with anything in particular. Later, as she was leaving to go to her room, Fräulein Rottenmeier called her into hers and stated that she was not to say "Grandmamma", and that when Frau Sesemann was with them she should always address her as "Gracious Madam". "Is that clear?" she concluded, as Heidi appeared puzzled, but the question was accompanied by such a look of finality that the girl sought no further explanation of the unfamiliar term.

Chapter 10

Grandmamma

T HE FOLLOWING EVENING the Sesemann household was visibly astir with expectation and preparation, and it was plain that the awaited lady wielded considerable influence and was held in great respect by everyone. Tinette had a brand-new white cap on her head, while Sebastian had collected all the footstools he could find and positioned them carefully so that wherever Frau Sesemann sat she would have one under her feet. Fräulein Rottenmeier walked stiffly from room to room to check everything was in order, as if to indicate that her own authority would not be extinguished by the approach of this sovereign power.

As the carriage drew up in front of the house, Sebastian and Tinette rushed down the porch steps. Fräulein Rottenmeier, knowing that she too must come forward to greet Frau Sesemann, followed at a more dignified pace.

Heidi had been told to go to her room and wait there till she was sent for; Frau Sesemann would doubtless wish to go to Klara first and have some moments alone with her. Heidi sat down in a corner and rehearsed the form of address she was to use. Before long, Tinette stuck her head round the door and, in her usual curt manner, said, "You're to go to the schoolroom."

Heidi had not felt able to ask Fräulein Rottenmeier if the form of address was really correct, but she thought that lady must have misspoken in saying "Gracious Madam", for she had only ever heard people say "Madam" and then a name. When she opened the schoolroom door, Frau Sesemann called out to her in a friendly voice: "Ah, this is the girl! Come here and let me have a good look at you."

Heidi walked over, and then she said in her clear voice, "Good day, Madam Gracious."

"Well, why not!" said Frau Sesemann laughingly. "Is that what people say in the Alps? Is that something you've heard back home?"

"No, no one says it there," replied Heidi gravely.

"Nor here!" And Frau Sesemann laughed again and patted Heidi on the cheek. "No matter. For the children I'm 'Grandmamma', and that's what you should call me. You can remember that, I suppose."

"Yes, very well. That's what I said before."

"Aha, I understand!" said Grandmamma, and she nodded her head in amusement. Then she looked at Heidi closely, nodding a few more times as she did so. Heidi stared earnestly into her eyes, and the kindliness she read in them gave her a warm feeling. Indeed she liked

Grandmamma's whole person so much that she could not avert her gaze. She had lovely white hair and a lace cap tied under her chin. Heidi was particularly struck by two broad ribbons attached to the cap that fluttered continually, as if Grandmamma always had a breeze around her.

"And what's your name, my child?" asked Grandmamma.

"It's just Heidi, but now it's supposed to be Adelheid, and so I'll try to…" She hesitated, feeling slightly guilty because she was not yet accustomed to the longer name and still did not answer when it was called out without warning by Fräulein Rottenmeier, who just then came into the room.

"I'm sure you'll agree, Frau Sesemann," she said, joining the others, "that I had to fix on a name that can be pronounced without awkwardness, not least for the servants' sakes."

"My dear Rottenmeier," replied Frau Sesemann, "if someone is called Heidi and is used to the name then that is what I'll call her – and there's an end to it."

Fräulein Rottenmeier was mortified that the old lady always addressed her by her surname alone. But there was nothing she could do: Grandmamma was set in her ways and could not be prevailed upon to change them. Furthermore, her powers of observation were as sharp as ever, and she had grasped the nature of the relationships in the house as soon as she entered it.

The day after her arrival, as Klara lay down for her usual afternoon rest, Grandmamma sat in the armchair next to her and shut her eyes for a few minutes. Then, soon refreshed, she rose to her feet and went into the dining room, which she found empty. "She's asleep," she said to herself. She walked over to Fräulein Rottenmeier's room and knocked loudly. After a while its occupant came to the door and, shocked at the sight of her unexpected visitor, started back a little.

"Where's the girl at this time of day, and what does she do? That's what I've come to ask," said Frau Sesemann.

"She sits in her room, where she could be usefully employed if only she had the least inclination for anything. But, Frau Sesemann, you just can't imagine what madcap stuff she thinks up and then actually carries through, things that are all but unmentionable in polite society."

"I would do the same if I had to sit alone like her, I can tell you, and you would find my stuff unmentionable in polite society too! Now, go and fetch the child and bring her to my sitting room. I'd like to give her a few pretty books I've brought along."

"But that's just it. That's the awful thing," exclaimed Fräulein Rottenmeier, clasping her hands. "What good are books to her? In all this time she hasn't even learnt the alphabet. It's impossible to give her the slightest notion of it, as the tutor can very well testify! And if that exemplary man didn't have the patience of a saint he would have given up teaching her long ago."

"Well, that is odd," said Frau Sesemann. "She doesn't look like the sort of child who can't learn the alphabet. Anyway, fetch her over. For now she can look at the pictures in the books."

Fräulein Rottenmeier had more to say, but Frau Sesemann turned away and hurried to her room. She was surprised to hear that Heidi was so backward and intended to look into the matter, though not when the tutor was present. She valued the tutor for his good character, but found his way of expressing himself somewhat ponderous, and whenever they met she greeted him with great warmth and then made off hastily in another direction to avoid getting caught up in a conversation with him.

Heidi joined Grandmamma in her sitting room and was filled with wonder by the gorgeous, brightly coloured illustrations in the large books she had brought with her. Suddenly, as the old lady turned the page to reveal a new picture, Heidi let out a cry. She stared at the picture with her eyes aglow, then she welled up with tears and began to sob violently. Grandmamma looked at the picture too. It showed a fine verdant pasture with various animals grazing and nibbling at the green bushes. In the midst of them stood a shepherd leaning on a long staff and surveying his merry flock. The scene was bathed in golden light, for the sun was just setting over the horizon.

Grandmamma took Heidi's hand in her own. "Come, come, my child," she said kindly. "Don't cry now! I suppose it reminded you of something. But look, there's a nice story to go with it, which I'll read you this evening. There are so many other nice stories in the book, all to read and retell. But first you and I must have a little talk together, so wipe away your tears. Good, now come and stand in front of me so I can have a good look at you. That's right, let's perk up again."

It was a while before Heidi could stop crying. Grandmamma gave her plenty of time to recover, and several times she spoke encouraging words: "There, that's better, now we can both feel happy again."

When the girl at last grew calm the old lady went on, "Now, I want you to tell me something, my child. How are you getting on in your lessons with the tutor? Are you learning and doing well?"

"Oh no," replied Heidi with a sigh, "but I knew beforehand it was too hard to learn."

"What's too hard to learn, Heidi? What do you mean?"

"I mean reading."

"Well, I never! And who told you that?"

"Peter. And he knows because he's had to try over and over again, but it's too hard and he just can't do it."

"Well then, Peter must be an odd character! But see, Heidi, you shouldn't simply accept everything a boy called Peter says. You should try for yourself. I'm certain you haven't really been concentrating when the tutor has shown you the letters of the alphabet."

"There's no point," said Heidi in a tone of complete resignation to the inevitable.

"Heidi," Grandmamma now began, "I want to tell you something. You've never learnt to read because you believed your Peter. But you should believe me instead when I tell you with absolute certainty that in a short space of time you will be able to read, just like a host of other children who have more in common with you than with Peter. And you must understand what reading will open up for you. You saw the shepherd on the beautiful green pasture. Well, once you can read I'll give you the book and you can find out his whole story, just as if someone were telling it to you – everything he does together with his sheep and goats and all the curious things that happen to him. You'd like to know that, Heidi, wouldn't you?"

Heidi listened with rapt attention. Her eyes shone as she took a deep breath and said, "Oh, if only I could read!"

"So you will, and it won't take long either, Heidi. I can see that already. But now we must look in on Klara. Come on, we'll take these pretty books with us." And Frau Sesemann held Heidi's hand and led her to the schoolroom.

Since the day she had tried to go home, when Fräulein Rottenmeier had scolded her on the stairs and said what wicked ingratitude it was to want to run away, and how fortunate that Herr Sesemann knew nothing about it, a change had taken place in Heidi. She had realized that, despite what her aunt had told her, she could not go home when she liked, and that instead she was to stay in Frankfurt for a long, long time, perhaps for good. Besides, she understood that Herr Sesemann would think it very ungrateful in her to want to leave, and imagined that Grandmamma and Klara would feel the same. Heidi did not want Grandmamma, who was so kind to her, to get angry, as Fräulein Rottenmeier had done, and so she could not tell a soul of her desire to go home. But her heart grew heavier, she lost her appetite and every day she looked a little paler.

At night she found it hard to fall asleep, for once she was alone and the house fell quiet it all came vividly to her mind's eye: the pastureland drenched in sunlight and the flowers. When she finally slept she dreamt of the red peaks of the Falknis and the fiery snowfield of the Schesaplana; and, on waking in the mornings, blissfully eager to run out of the cottage, she suddenly saw that she was in her big bed in Frankfurt, so very far from home and with no chance of getting there. Then she buried her face in the pillow and cried and cried, but softly so that no one heard her.

Heidi's loss of spirits did not escape Grandmamma's notice. She let a few days go by to see if her air of dejection would lift, but it did not, and some mornings she perceived that she had been weeping. Therefore she took the girl into her sitting room one day, set her in front of herself, and said in a gentle voice, "Now tell me what's wrong, Heidi. Is something troubling you?"

Grandmamma had always been so kind that the last thing Heidi wanted was to show ingratitude, which might make her less kind in future. So, in a sad voice, she said, "I can't talk about it."

"Can't you? Could you talk about it to Klara?"

"No, not to anyone!" said Heidi firmly, and she looked so wretched that the old lady felt deeply sorry for her.

"Come, my child," she said, "let me tell you something. If you have troubles you can't talk about to anyone, you should open your heart to God and seek His guidance. He can relieve us of all the sorrows that weigh us down. You do know that, don't you? I expect you pray every night to God in Heaven and give thanks for His blessings and ask Him to protect you from harm."

"No, I don't do that," the child replied.

"Have you never prayed, Heidi? Do you know what prayer is?"

"I've only ever prayed with the other grandmother, but that was a long time ago and I've forgotten how to do it."

"Well, Heidi, that's why you feel sad – you don't know anyone who can help you. Just think what a comfort it must be when your heart is constantly aching and oppressed that you can turn to God at any moment and tell Him everything and ask for the help no one else can give you! And He can always help and make you feel happy again."

Heidi's eyes gleamed with joy: "Can I really tell Him everything?"

"Yes, Heidi, everything."

The girl withdrew her hand, which Grandmamma had held between hers, and said hastily: "May I go now?"

"Of course you may!" came the reply, and Heidi ran across to her room, sat on a stool and folded her hands. Then she poured out all her woe to the Good Lord and begged Him earnestly to help her by letting her go home to Grandfather.

A little more than a week after this, the tutor requested permission to wait on Frau Sesemann. Something peculiar had taken place, and he wished to discuss it with her. He was called to her sitting room, and on seeing him enter Frau Sesemann cordially held out her hand: "I'm so glad to see you! Do come and sit here by me." She arranged a chair for him. "Now tell me, what would you like to speak to me about? I trust nothing has happened to upset you."

"On the contrary, Madam," he began, "something has occurred that I had given up hoping for, indeed that nobody in any way familiar with what had gone before could have foreseen, something that it was logical to suppose was quite out of the question and yet has now in a most wonderful manner come to pass, apparently negating everything that normal processes of reasoning would lead one to expect—"

"Has Heidi learnt to read, by any chance?" Frau Sesemann interjected.

He looked at her, speechless with astonishment. "It really is quite marvellous," he said at last, "not only that the girl had previously been unable to learn the alphabet, despite my most unremitting endeavours and detailed explanations, but also, and more particularly, that after I had resolved to accept the unattainability of the goal, leave off any further elucidations and merely place the letters before her in their bare state, as it were, she in a very short space of time – one might indeed say overnight – developed the ability to read, articulating the words with a clarity I have rarely encountered in beginners. And almost as marvellous to me as the unlikely fact itself is the knowledge that you, Madam, entertained the possibility of it."

"Well, human beings are capable of the strangest things," declared Frau Sesemann with a contented smile. "Sometimes, too, one element combines happily with another, such as an ambition to learn with a new teaching method, both good things in themselves. So let us rejoice that the child has come this far and hope her progress continues."

With that she accompanied the tutor to the door and then hurried to the schoolroom to assure herself that this pleasing report was true. It appeared to be, for there sat

Heidi next to Klara reading her a story, and doing so with visibly increasing wonder and enthusiasm, stepping into the world now open to her, as the black letters burst into life in the form of touching stories of people and places.

That evening, as they sat down to dinner, Heidi found on her plate the big book with the beautiful pictures. She turned her questioning eyes to Grandmamma, who said, with a friendly nod, "Yes, it's yours now."

"To keep? Even when I go home?" asked Heidi, flushing with pleasure.

"Yes, of course!" Grandmamma confirmed. "Tomorrow we'll start reading it."

"But you won't be going home, Heidi, not for years yet," Klara interjected. "And when Grandmamma goes away again I'll need you even more."

Heidi could not go to bed without looking into her handsome book, and from that day forward her favourite occupation was sitting with it open in front of her and reading the stories that went with the lovely, colourful pictures. She was delighted when Grandmamma said of an evening, "Let's have Heidi read to us," for she could now do so without difficulty. The stories seemed much better and clearer when she read them aloud, and Grandmamma would explain many things and add more information of her own.

Best of all, Heidi liked looking at the picture of the green pasture and the shepherd standing among the animals, looking so cheerful as he leant on his long staff. At this point he was still with his father's fine flock and enjoying the companionship of the sheep and goats. This was followed by the picture after he had run away from the family home and was living abroad, obliged to look after pigs and very thin from getting nothing but spent grain to eat. In this picture the sun had lost its golden glow, and the scene was grey and misty. But then came the final illustration to the story: the old father emerging from his house with outstretched arms and running to welcome his penitent son, who wore a ragged jacket and looked fearful and emaciated as he approached his old home. This was the story Heidi liked best. She was forever reading it, aloud or in an undertone, and she never tired of hearing Grandmamma explain its meaning to her and Klara. There were many other good stories in the book, and reading them and looking at the pictures made the days race by till it was nearly time for Grandmamma to leave them.

Chapter 11

Heidi Grows in Mind, but Not in Body

E VERY AFTERNOON OF HER VISIT, as Klara lay
down and Fräulein Rottenmeier, presumably in need
of rest, vanished without explanation, Grandmamma
would settle herself next to Klara and close her eyes. No
more than five minutes later she was invariably on her
feet again and calling Heidi over to her sitting room for
a chat and to keep her busy and entertained in various
ways. She had some pretty dolls and showed Heidi how
to make dresses and aprons for them, so that she learnt to
sew without realizing it and made very attractive coats and
other clothes for the little figures using the richly coloured
pieces of material Grandmamma always had to hand.
Now that Heidi could do so, Grandmamma very often
let her read one of her stories aloud. This was a treat for
the girl, who liked the stories better and better the more

she read them. She entered into the characters' lives and felt a close relationship with them all, rejoicing each time she was among them again.

Despite all this, Heidi never looked truly happy, and her eyes had lost their old sparkle. One day in the final week of Grandmamma's stay in Frankfurt she was called to her room as usual while Klara was sleeping. As she walked in, the big book under her arm, Grandmamma waved her over to where she was sitting, laid the book down and said, "Now tell me, my child, why are you sad? Do you still have the same sorrow?"

Heidi nodded.

"And have you opened your heart to God?"

"Yes."

"Do you pray to Him daily to make everything right so you can be happy again?"

"No, I don't pray at all any more."

"But Heidi, I can't believe my ears! Why on earth not?"

"It was no use. God did not listen, and I think I know why." Heidi's voice quickened as she spoke. "When so, so many people in Frankfurt are praying in the evening at the same time, God can't pay attention to them all. I'm sure He didn't even hear me."

"But how can you know that, Heidi?"

"Because every day I asked for the same thing, week after week, and God did not answer my prayer."

"That's not how it works, Heidi! Don't think of it like that. Listen, God is a loving father to us all, and He always knows what is best for us – even when we don't. If we want something from Him that is not good for us, He doesn't grant it. Instead, He grants us something much better, but only if we carry on praying to Him sincerely, not if we give up and lose our trust in Him. So, you see, what you requested was not right for you at that time. The good Lord heard you well enough. He can hear and consider everyone at once, you see, because He isn't a mere mortal like you or me. And because He knew what was good for you, He thought to himself: yes, Heidi shall have what she desires, but only at a time when it is good for her, so that she can really rejoice in it. If I give her what she wants now, she will see afterwards that it would have been better for me to deny her, and she will weep and say, 'If only the good Lord had refused my request, which doesn't at all benefit me as I thought it would.' And while God was watching over you to see whether you placed your trust in Him, whether you offered up daily prayers and looked to Him when you were in need, you turned your face from Him and lost your faith. You ceased praying and forgot the good Lord altogether. But, you see, when someone does this, and God no longer hears that person's voice among the prayerful, so He forgets him too and lets him choose his own path. But if he then falls into hardship and laments that he receives no help, nobody will pity him, rather they will all say: 'You turned your face from God who might have helped you!' Is that what you want for yourself, Heidi, or do you want to return to the good Lord and beg His forgiveness that you turned away from Him, and then pray each day and trust Him to do what is best for you, so that your heart is filled with gladness again?"

Heidi listened very carefully. Every word Grandmamma spoke pierced her heart, for she trusted the old lady implicitly. "I want to go and ask God's forgiveness straight away, and I won't forget Him again," she said contritely.

"That's right, my child. And He will help you at the appropriate time – never fear!" Grandmamma assured her.

Heidi ran straight to her room and prayed with earnest remorse to the good Lord and begged Him to watch over her again and not to forget her.

The day of Grandmamma's departure came, and a sad one it was for Klara and Heidi. But the kind old lady organized everything in such a way as to banish all mournfulness; rather it was like a special holiday until the moment she drove away in the carriage. Afterwards the house seemed silent and empty, as if the life had gone from it, and for the rest of the day Klara and Heidi sat looking lost, not knowing what to do with themselves.

The next day, during the time after their lessons that the girls usually spent together, Heidi came into the schoolroom carrying her book and said, "Now I always want to read to you, Klara. Is that all right?"

For the moment Klara was happy to assent to this, and Heidi launched eagerly into her self-appointed task. But she did not get very far before coming to a complete stop. She had just begun a story about a dying grandmother, when suddenly she called out, "Oh, now Grandmother is dead!" and broke down and cried pitifully. Everything Heidi read was utterly real to her, and she felt convinced it was Peter's grandmother who had died. Amid her sobs she wailed, "Now Grandmother is dead, and I'll never be able to visit her again, and she didn't get a single bread roll!"

Klara explained at length to Heidi that it was not Peter's grandmother who had died, but a quite different person who was the subject of the story. Even after the shaken girl was finally brought to an understanding of this, she did not calm down, but carried on weeping inconsolably, for the idea had taken root in her mind that Grandmother could die while she herself was so far away – and Grandfather too – so that when she returned to the mountains after a long absence she might find everyone dead and gone, leaving her all alone and never again to see those she loved.

During this exchange Fräulein Rottenmeier came into the room and heard Klara trying to make Heidi perceive her error. Seeing Heidi still unable to stop sobbing, she strode with visible irritation towards the girls.

"Adelheid, that's enough of this senseless racket!" she said sternly. "Let me tell you this: if ever you indulge in another such outburst while reading your stories I'll take the book off you and you won't get it back."

Her words had their effect, for the book was Heidi's greatest treasure. Turning white with terror, she hastily dried her eyes and swallowed hard to stifle her sobs, so that not a sound was heard from her. Nor did these words lose their force. Whatever Heidi went on to read, she shed no tears over it, although sometimes the effort needed to refrain from voicing her dismay was so obvious that Klara exclaimed, "Heidi, you're pulling such dreadful faces. I've never seen anything like it." However, her grimaces, making no noise, escaped Fräulein Rottenmeier's notice, and as she fought off each spell of harrowing sadness without a murmur everything went on smoothly. But she quite lost her appetite and looked very pale and thin, and Sebastian, pained by the change, could hardly bear to watch as Heidi let the choicest morsels set before her pass untasted. Often he would coax her in an undertone as he held out a dish to her: "Take some of this, little miss – it's excellent. Not like that, a proper helping – and another." But neither this nor all his other fatherly urging did any good. Heidi scarcely ate anything, and when she went to bed at night images from home flooded her mind and filled her with longing, and she cried softly into her pillow so that no one would hear.

Months passed and, as the walls and windows she saw from all sides of the Sesemann residence never changed, Heidi had no idea if it was summer or winter. She only went outside on the rare occasions Klara was strong enough to be taken for a drive, and these excursions were very brief, as she could only stand the motion of the carriage for short periods. They generally did not get beyond the walls and stone-paved streets, but rather turned back and continued through wide, handsome thoroughfares where there were plenty of houses and people on view, but no grass and flowers, no fir trees and no mountains. Heidi's yearning for the sight of beautiful, familiar objects increased with each passing day, and merely reading the word for one of them stoked her memory and caused a burst of pain that she needed all her strength to overcome.

Autumn and winter went by, and when the sun started beating down on the white walls of the house opposite

Heidi knew it would soon be time for Peter to return to the pastureland with the goats, and that the golden rock roses would glitter in the sunshine and the surrounding mountains would be ablaze every evening. She sat in a corner of her lonely room and covered her eyes with her hands so as not to see the wall reflecting the sunlight. There she remained, silent and motionless, battling her burning homesickness, until Klara called for her.

Chapter 12

Haunted House

F OR A FEW DAYS Fräulcin Rottenmeier had generally been subdued and taciturn as she went about the house. If the light was fading as she walked down the long corridor from one room to another she often peered left and right, into the recesses, and even quickly behind her, as if she thought someone might creep up on her and pluck at her dress. Indeed, she only moved on her own among the rooms in everyday use. If her duties took her to the elegantly furnished guest bedrooms on the upper floor or to the grand, eerie state room on the ground floor, in which her every step echoed loudly and the old councillors with their broad white collars and big, grave eyes stared down intently from the walls, she now always summoned Tinette to her side on the pretext that something might need to be carried up or down.

Tinette did exactly the same herself: if she had anything to see to on the upper or lower floors she called for Sebastian to accompany her, because there might be something to fetch that was too heavy for her. Oddly enough, Sebastian's policy was no different: if he was sent to a remote part of the house, he brought Johann up and made him go with him in case he could not get whatever was wanted without help. And each of them was a willing escort, although there was never anything to carry and a single person would always have been enough. Seemingly everyone's first thought on being asked to accompany another was that they might soon need that person to perform the same service for them. Meanwhile, the long-serving cook stood pensively among her pots and pans in the basement, shook her head and sighed: "I never thought I'd live to see the day!"

The fact was that for a while now there had been some strange and uncanny goings-on in Herr Sesemann's house. Each morning, when the servants came downstairs, they found the front door wide open, but no one anywhere in sight that might be responsible for opening it. The first few days this occurred the inhabitants of the house took fright and made a thorough search of its rooms to see what had been stolen, the assumption being that a burglar had managed to hide somewhere and then made off in the night with his booty. But nothing had been taken; not one object was missing from any part of the property. At night the door was double-bolted, and for good measure a thick wooden bar was placed across it – to no avail: next morning it was open again. Regardless of how early the alarmed servants came down together they were met with the same sight, even though everyone in the neighbourhood was still fast asleep and the doors and windows of their houses were firmly shut. Eventually Johann and Sebastian, under strong pressure from Fräulein Rottenmeier, plucked up their courage and braced themselves to pass a night in the room adjoining the state room and keep watch. The housekeeper sought out some weapons belonging to Herr Sesemann and handed Sebastian a large bottle of spirits, providing him and Johann with the means to fortify and defend themselves as required.

The two men filled their posts on the appointed night and soon began taking liquid sustenance, which made them very talkative at first and sleepy afterwards. They both reclined in their chairs, and their voices fell silent. When the nearby old church clock struck midnight, Sebastian pulled himself together and called out to his companion. Johann was not easy to rouse, however, and at the sound of his name he merely rolled his head from one side of the backrest to the other and slept on. Sebastian was now wide awake, and he listened keenly; there was no sound anywhere, not even from the street outside. He did not drop off to sleep again, because the eerie stillness made him very uneasy, and he merely hissed softly at Johann and gave him a little shake now and then. Finally, as the clock struck one, Johann woke up and recollected why he was sitting in a chair rather then lying in his bed. Then he shot bravely to his feet and declared, "Now, Sebastian, we'd better go outside and see how things look. Don't be afraid. Just follow me!"

Johann opened the door of the room – which had been left ajar – and, with Sebastian just behind him, stepped into the hall. At that instant a sharp gust of air blew in from the open front door and snuffed out the light in his hand. He hurtled back, almost throwing Sebastian across the room, then hauled him back to the door of the room, which he slammed shut. With feverish haste he turned the key in the lock as far as it would go and then snatched his matches from his pocket and relit the candle. Sebastian had little idea what had happened, Johann's bulky form having largely shielded him from the gust. But at the sight of him now by candlelight, deathly white and trembling like a leaf, he yelped with fear.

"What's out there? What did you see?" he asked eagerly.

"The door completely open," gasped Johann, "and a white figure mounting the stairs and then gone in a flash!"

A shiver ran down Sebastian's spine. The two men pushed their chairs up against each other and sat without moving until day broke and people began to stir in the street outside. Then they left the room together, closed the gaping front door and went upstairs to inform Fräulein Rottenmeier of the night's events. She was already up and dressed, her sleep having been interrupted by the expectation of their report. As soon as she learnt what had happened, she sat down to write a letter to Herr Sesemann unlike any he had ever received. In it she told him her fingers were numb with fear. She spoke of outrageous goings-on and pressed him to make immediate arrangements for his return and to set off without delay. Then she related the previous night's events and said that the front door still stood open each morning. In these circumstances everyone in the house felt their lives to be in peril and none could foresee the terrible consequences these sinister proceedings might have.

Herr Sesemann replied by return of post that it was impossible for him to drop everything and come straight home. The ghost story was most disconcerting, he went on, and he hoped it might soon be concluded. However, if things did not settle down, Fräulein Rottenmeier should write to his mother and ask her to come to Frankfurt to help them. Frau Sesemann would doubtless make short work of any ghosts, and it would be a while before they dared disturb the peace in his house again.

Fräulein Rottenmeier was dissatisfied with the tone of this letter, which suggested he was taking the matter too lightly. She fired off another letter to Frau Sesemann, but the response from this quarter was no more acceptable and contained some pointed remarks. Frau Sesemann wrote that she did not intend to make a special journey from Holstein to Frankfurt because Fräulein Rottenmeier had seen a ghost. In any case, no such apparition had ever been spotted in the Sesemann residence before, and if there was one stalking the place now it must be a living being, with whom her correspondent ought to be able to reach an accommodation. If not, she should request the assistance of the nightwatchman.

But Fräulein Rottenmeier, who was resolved not to go on living in terror, had another plan. As yet she had said nothing of the ghost to the two girls, thinking they would be too frightened to accept being left alone by day or night, which could cause her no little inconvenience. Now, though, she went straight to the schoolroom, where they were sitting together, and told them in hushed tones about the mysterious nocturnal visitor. Klara shrieked that she would not spend another second alone, and that Papa must come home, and that Fräulein Rottenmeier must sleep in her room, and that Heidi must never be on her own either in case the ghost found her and harmed her. All three would stay in the same room with the light burning through the night, she said, and Tinette would sleep in the next room, and Sebastian and Johann would spend the night in the corridor, so that they could call out if the ghost came up the stairs and scare it off.

Klara was very upset, and Fräulein Rottenmeier had the greatest difficulty in calming her down. She promised to write to her father at once, to move her bed into her room and not to leave her alone any more. She said they could not all sleep in the same room, but if Adelheid was afraid Tinette would set up a bed for herself in her room. However, Heidi was more afraid of Tinette than of ghosts – whose existence she had never heard of – and she quickly said she did not feel worried and was content to be by herself in her room. Thereupon Fräulein Rottenmeier hastened to her desk and wrote to Herr Sesemann that the uncanny incidents occurring in the house night after night had so shattered his daughter's fragile health that the gravest dangers were to be apprehended. In similar cases there had been sudden episodes of epileptic seizures or St Vitus's dance, and without the removal of whatever was terrorizing the household the risk to Klara was great.

The tactic worked. Two days later Herr Sesemann stood before his own front door and pulled the bell so hard that the servants all scurried together and stared at one another, convinced the ghost was now brazenly playing its malicious tricks before nightfall. Sebastian peered down warily at the porch through a half-open shutter, and as he did so there was another ring of the bell, this time so emphatic that they all instinctively felt a vigorous human hand must be at work. Indeed, Sebastian had recognized that hand, and he dashed through the room, tumbled down the stairs, quickly straightened himself out and yanked open the door. Herr Sesemann passed him with a brief nod and went straight up to his daughter's room. Klara received her Papa with whoops of joy, and his deeply furrowed brow was smoothed as he beheld her so cheerful and otherwise unchanged. His face lit up further when she told him she was as well as ever and delighted he had come home, and that she now liked the ghost that was haunting the house better for being the cause of her Papa's return.

"And what else has the ghost been up to, Fräulein Rottenmeier?" he asked, his lips twitching into a smile.

"It's no laughing matter, Herr Sesemann," that lady responded earnestly. "I doubt you will still consider it a joke tomorrow, because what's going on indicates that this house harbours some dreadful secrets from times gone by."

"Well, I know nothing of that," remarked Herr Sesemann, "but I must beg you not to cast aspersions on my wholly respectable ancestors. Now, please send Sebastian to the dining room. I want a word with him alone."

It had not escaped his notice that there was little love lost between Sebastian and Fräulein Rottenmeier, and this gave him an idea. The servant appeared just after Herr Sesemann had gone into the dining room, and he waved him over.

"Come here, Sebastian. I have a question that needs an honest answer. Have you perhaps been doing some ghostly play-acting to keep Fräulein Rottenmeier entertained, hey?"

"No, upon my honour, sir, you mustn't think that. I feel pretty queasy about the whole business myself," answered Sebastian. His sincerity was plain to see.

"Well, in that case I'll show you and the gallant Johann how ghosts look by daylight. You ought to be ashamed, a strapping lad like you, to run away from a ghost! Now, you're to go this instant to my old friend Dr Classen. Give him my compliments, and ask him to come to this house at nine o'clock tonight without fail. Say I have made the journey from Paris specially to consult him. It's so serious he'll have to sit up with me all night, and he should make his arrangements. Is that clear, Sebastian?"

"Indeed it is, sir. I'll repeat exactly what you've said."

Sebastian left the room, and Herr Sesemann returned to his daughter to allay her fears, telling her that in the hours ahead he meant to clear up the whole mystery.

At the stroke of nine, just after the girls had gone to bed and Fräulein Rottenmeier had retired for the night, Dr Classen arrived. He had a fresh-complexioned face framed by grey hair and bright, kind eyes. On coming in he looked anxious, but after greeting his friend he burst out laughing.

"Well, old chap, for someone who needs a bedside vigil you don't look too bad!" he said, clapping him on the shoulder.

"Just you wait, old chap," Herr Sesemann replied. "The real object of the vigil will look bad enough once we've captured him."

"Are you saying someone is sick here, then, and needs to be captured as well?"

"It's worse than that, doctor, much worse. There's a ghost! My house is haunted!"

Dr Classen laughed loudly again.

"Is that your bedside manner, doctor?" Herr Sesemann continued. "A shame my friend Fräulein Rottenmeier isn't here to appreciate it. She's convinced one of my ancestors is rumbling around the house doing penance for terrible crimes."

"And how did she make his acquaintance?" asked Dr Classen, still highly amused.

Herr Sesemann related the whole sequence of events and told him that for a while now someone had been opening the front door during the night, as the entire household had testified. He added that to be prepared for every eventuality he had placed two fully loaded revolvers where they were to keep watch. The whole thing might be a misplaced practical joke played by an acquaintance of one of the servants to frighten everyone in the house in the master's absence – in which case scaring him by firing over his head might bring him to his senses. A second possibility was that thieves were trying to create the impression of a ghost in people's minds to ensure they didn't venture from their rooms at night – and in that case too a good weapon could come in handy.

As he spoke, the two men went down the stairs and into the room in which Johann and Sebastian had spent the night. On the table stood a few bottles of good wine, for should they have to stay there till morning a little occasional refreshment would certainly be welcome. Beside the bottles were the revolvers, and in the middle of the table two branched candlesticks that gave out a strong light, Herr Sesemann not quite having the nerve to sit waiting for the ghost in semi-darkness.

The door was left open just a crack, because too much light seeping into the hallway could put the ghost off. The men settled comfortably into their armchairs and began exchanging anecdotes, taking a draught of wine now and again, and before they knew it the clock struck midnight.

"The ghost has probably got wind of us and won't come tonight," the doctor said.

"Wait a bit. Apparently it tends to come around one o'clock," replied his friend.

They fell back into their conversation. By the time the clock struck one, the streets were empty and there was no sound anywhere in the vicinity. Suddenly Dr Classen raised his finger: "Hush! Sesemann, can you hear it?"

They both listened. Softly but distinctly, they heard the wooden bar sliding off the door, the key turning twice in the lock and the door opening. Herr Sesemann reached for his revolver.

"You aren't afraid, are you?" said the doctor, rising from his chair.

"Just a precaution," whispered Herr Sesemann. Each took a candlestick in his left hand and a revolver in his right, and the doctor led the way into the hall. The pallid moonlight was flooding through the open front door, illuminating a white figure that stood motionless on the threshold.

"Who's there?" bellowed the doctor, making the hall resound with his voice, and the two men, holding their weapons and lights, advanced towards the figure. It turned and gave a little cry. Barefoot in her white nightgown, staring in bewilderment at the bright flames and the weapons, trembling and shaking all over like a leaf in the wind, was Heidi. The men stared at each other in disbelief.

"Why, Sesemann, I believe it's your little water-carrier," said Dr Classen.

"What's the meaning of this, child?" asked Herr Sesemann. "What are you doing? Why have you come downstairs?"

Heidi stood before him, white with fear. "I don't know," she said faintly.

The doctor stepped forward. "This is my department, Sesemann. Go back and sit in your chair. I'll take the girl to her room."

Having placed his revolver on the floor, he held the quivering girl protectively by the hand and led her to the stairs. "Don't be afraid, don't be afraid," he said kindly as they went up together. "Just keep calm. There's nothing at all to worry about."

On entering Heidi's room, Dr Classen set his light down on the table, lifted Heidi into bed and carefully pulled the covers over her. Then he sat in the chair beside the bed and waited for the trembling in her limbs to cease. Once she was calmer, he folded his hand over hers and said soothingly, "Everything is fine now. Tell me, where were you going?"

"Nowhere, I'm sure," insisted Heidi. "I didn't even go downstairs. I was just suddenly there."

"I see. And did you have any dreams tonight? Did you see or hear anything clearly in them?"

"Yes, I have the same dream every night. I'm with Grandfather, and outside I can hear the wind whistling through the fir trees, and I think: now the stars will be shining so brightly in the sky. And I go down quickly to open the door of the cottage, and it's all so lovely! But when I wake up I'm always in Frankfurt."

And Heidi swallowed hard and fought back the pressure building up in her throat.

"Hmm. And do you feel pain anywhere? In your head or your back?"

"No, just a big weight here, like a stone."

"Hmm. You mean like when you've eaten something and you wish you could bring it back up again?"

"No, just the feeling when you want to cry very much."

"And do you sometimes have a good cry?"

"On no, that's not allowed! Fräulein Rottenmeier said so."

"So you swallow it down each time, is that it? I see. But you like being in Frankfurt, don't you?"

"Oh, yes." The answer seemed contradicted by the smallness of the voice that uttered it.

"Hmm. And where did you live with your grandfather?"

"Always on the mountainside."

"Well, I suppose that's not much fun. Probably a bit dull, isn't it?"

"No, it's beautiful there, just beautiful!" Heidi's voice faltered. The remembrance of home, the excitement she had just gone through and the long-repressed urge to cry overwhelmed her resistance. Unstoppable tears welled from her eyes and she broke into loud, bitter sobbing.

The doctor got up and gently laid Heidi's head down on the pillow, saying, "There, you have a little cry. It will do you no harm. And then have a nice, deep sleep. All will be well in the morning."

He left her and returned to the downstairs room where his friend was anxiously waiting to hear his report. Dr Classen sat in the armchair opposite him and began to speak: "Well, Sesemann, first of all your young charge is a sleep-walker. She has quite unwittingly been imitating a ghost by opening your front door night after night and reducing your entire domestic staff to quivering jellies. Secondly, she's so homesick that she's wasting away, and the bones poking through her skin may soon be all that's left of her. Something must be done at once! For the first condition, which is a symptom of extreme nervous agitation, there is only one remedy, which is to restore the girl directly to her native mountain air. For the second condition too there is but a single cure, which is precisely the same. She must leave for home tomorrow – that's my prescription."

Herr Sesemann rose to his feet in consternation and paced up and down the room.

"Sleepwalking, homesick, ill!" he exclaimed. "Wasting away here in my house and no one realizes or takes any notice! And now, doctor, you tell me to send a child who arrived here hale and hearty back to her grandfather miserable and emaciated. No, you can't ask that of me. I can't, I won't do it. Take the girl into your care straight away and give her any treatment you like to make her well again. Then I'll send her home if she wants to go. But first I need your help!"

"Just think what you're proposing, Sesemann," replied the doctor gravely. "This isn't a bodily disorder than can be cured with powders and pills. The girl has a sound constitution, and if you send her back to the healthy mountain air that she's used to she should make a full recovery. If you don't… I can't believe you want her grandfather to get her back mortally ill, or not at all."

Shocked, Herr Sesemann stood still.

"Well, doctor, if you put it like that, there's only one thing to be done, and without delay."

As he spoke his took his friend's arm and wandered back and forth with him to discuss the necessary arrangements. Then Dr Classen made ready to go home. It had been a long visit, and as he went out through the front door – opened this time by the master of the house – the first rays of dawn penetrated the hall.

Chapter 13

A Summer Evening Homecoming

Herr sesemann climbed the stairs in great per-
turbation and marched up to Fräulein Rottenmeier's
bedroom. He knocked on the door with such unwonted
force that she awoke instantly and shot up in bed with
a shriek. She could hear her employer's voice outside:
"Please come to the dining room as quickly as you can.
We need to make immediate preparations for a journey."

Fräulein Rottenmeier looked at her clock: half-past four
in the morning. Never in her life had she got up so early.
What could have happened? In her curiosity and trepida-
tion she struggled to dress, fumbling with her clothes and
rushing madly round the room in search of garments she
had already put on.

Meanwhile Herr Sesemann went farther up the corridor and yanked with all his strength at the bells that

communicated with the servants' bedrooms, causing their terrified occupants to leap from their beds and throw on their clothes in confusion. They all thought the ghost must have set about the master and this was his cry for help. So they came down one by one and presented themselves, each more dishevelled than the last, and were astounded to find him striding briskly up and down the dining room in apparently good spirits, not at all like a man who has just had a nasty brush with a ghost. He sent Johann straight out to see to the carriage and horses and draw them up in front of the house; he instructed Tinette to wake Heidi and get her dressed and ready for a journey; and he told Sebastian to hurry to the house where Heidi's aunt was in service and fetch her over.

By this time Fräulein Rottenmeier had managed to get her clothes on, with everything correctly adjusted except her cap, which was the wrong way round and, from a distance, made it look as if she were facing backwards. Herr Sesemann put this odd appearance down to the effects of an unfinished night's sleep and got straight down to business. He directed her to find a trunk at once and pack it with everything belonging to the Swiss girl – this was what he generally called Heidi, whose name sat awkwardly on his tongue – together with a selection of Klara's clothes, so that she went home reasonably well provided for. It had to be done fast, he said, without mulling over each item.

But Fräulein Rottenmeier was frozen to the spot, staring at Herr Sesemann in blank astonishment. She had assumed he wished to confide in her the hair-raising story of his night-time encounter with the ghost, which now in the full light of morning she would not have been averse to hearing. Instead he had given her a thoroughly mundane and disagreeable task. It was all too unexpected to be digested quickly. She stood stock-still, waiting to see what would come next.

Herr Sesemann, however, had no mind to explain himself further. He left her where she was and went to his daughter's room. As he suspected, Klara had been woken by the unusual stirrings in the house and was listening intently, trying to puzzle out what was going on around her. Her father sat by her bed and told her how the truth about the ghost had come to light. The doctor had pronounced Heidi's health to be precarious, he said, and believed she was likely to extend her nocturnal wanderings little by little and possibly even get on the roof, which would be extremely dangerous. Hence his decision to send her home immediately. He could not take the risk of something happening and hoped Klara would understand that no other course was possible and would reconcile herself to the change.

This news came as a painful surprise to Klara, who at first cast around for alternatives. But it was no good: her father had made up his mind. He did, though, promise to take her to Switzerland the following year as long as she was sensible and did not make a fuss. So Klara resigned herself to the inevitable, only requesting that the trunk be brought into her room and packed there so that she could add in whatever she liked. To this he gladly agreed; indeed he encouraged her to put together a good stock of clothes for Heidi.

By now Dete had arrived and stood in keen anticipation in the hall, for such an early summons meant there had to be something exceptional going on. Herr Sesemann went out to her and said how things were with Heidi and that he desired her to take the child home that very day. Dete was highly disappointed – this was not what she had expected. Besides, she clearly remembered the Alp Uncle's parting words to her that he never wanted to see her again, and having brought Heidi to him and taken her away again it did not seem a good idea to bring her back to him now.

After a brief pause for these reflections she explained with great eloquence that it would be impossible for her to travel that day, that the next day would be even more out of the question, and the days after that most impossible of all, because of the many jobs she had to do. Looking further ahead, she would be even busier. Herr Sesemann understood the true meaning of her words and dismissed her without further ado. Then he sent for Sebastian and told him to prepare himself at once for a journey. He was to go as far as Basel that evening and then take the girl home the following day before coming straight back. There would be no message for him to convey: it would all be in a letter addressed to the girl's grandfather.

"But there's one important thing you mustn't forget, Sebastian!" he continued. "I've written the name of a Basel hotel on this business card. I'm known there, so if you present the card they'll give you a good room for the girl, and you'll no doubt find reasonable quarters for yourself too. Then go into the girl's room and fasten all the windows so securely that they can only be opened with great force, and once she's in bed lock her door on the outside. She walks in her sleep and might get into danger in an unfamiliar building if she wandered about and maybe tried to open the front door. Is that clear?"

"Oh, so that's what it was?" cried Sebastian in amazement. A light had just come on in his head regarding the ghostly visitations.

"Yes, that's what it was! Just so! And you're a big ninny, and you can tell Johann he's one too and the whole lot of you a pack of fools."

With that Herr Sesemann went into his study, where he sat at his desk and wrote a letter to the Alp Uncle.

Sebastian was too astounded to move from the middle of the room. He kept repeating to himself: "If only I hadn't let that coward Johann yank me back from the door that night. I could have gone after the figure in white, as I certainly would now!" These thoughts were reinforced by the bright sunlight penetrating every corner of the dove-grey room.

Meanwhile Heidi, in her Sunday dress, was standing in her bedroom wondering what was going to happen. Tinette had shaken her out of her sleep, taken her clothes from the wardrobe and helped her on with them, all in silence. She thought the uneducated child beneath her notice and never wasted any words on her.

With his letter between his fingers Herr Sesemann walked into the dining room, where breakfast was on the table. "Where's the girl?" he called out.

Heidi was fetched, and as she approached to wish him a good morning he gave her a questioning look: "Well, poppet, what do you think of our plan?"

She looked up at him in surprise.

"I see no one has told you," he laughed. "You're going home. Going home today."

"Home?" she repeated in a flat voice, turning quite pale. She felt something clutch at her heart and for a few seconds could not breathe.

"Or perhaps you don't want to," said a smiling Herr Sesemann.

"Oh, but I do!" said Heidi, turning a deep shade of red.

"Very well," he said encouragingly. He sat down and motioned to her to do likewise. "And now let's get a good breakfast inside you and then into the carriage and away!"

But Heidi could not swallow a morsel, try as she might to oblige him. She was in such a state of excitement that she did not know if it was all a dream and she might once more wake up in her nightgown standing next to the front door.

"Tell Sebastian to take plenty of food with him," Herr Sesemann instructed Fräulein Rottenmeier, who had just come in. "She can't eat anything at the moment, which is understandable." Turning to Heidi, he said kindly, "Go and wait with Klara till the carriage is brought round."

This was just what Heidi wanted, and she ran to Klara's room. There, in the middle of the floor, she saw an immense trunk with the lid thrown back.

"Come in, Heidi, come in," Klara called out. "Look what I've had packed for you! What do you think?"

She gave a list of different items: dresses, aprons, hand-kerchiefs, sewing things. "And look here," she added, hold-ing a basket triumphantly in the air. Heidi peered into it and jumped for joy, for it held a dozen lovely plump white rolls, all for Grandmother. In their delight the girls forgot that the moment of parting was imminent, and when they heard the words "The carriage is ready" shouted up from below there was no time for sorrow. Heidi dashed into her room to find Grandmamma's beautiful book, which nobody could have packed because she had kept it under her pillow so as not to be separated from it even while she slept. She laid it over the rolls in the basket and then opened the wardrobe in search of another cherished possession that had perhaps been overlooked. And there it was, the red scarf, which Fräulein Rottenmeier had not thought worth packing. Heidi wrapped it round something else to make a bright-red parcel and placed it eye-catchingly on top of the basket's other contents. Then she put on her pretty hat and left the room.

The girls had to say their goodbyes hurriedly, since Herr Sesemann was already waiting to take Heidi to the carriage. Fräulein Rottenmeier stood at the head of the stairs to bid Heidi farewell, and when she caught sight of the curious red bundle she snatched it from the basket and threw it on the floor. "No, Adelheid," she scolded, "you can't set off from this house with that thing. What can you possibly want with it? Goodbye!"

Heidi could not disobey her and pick up the bundle, but she looked beseechingly at the master of the house, as if her greatest treasure were being taken from her.

"No, no," said Herr Sesemann authoritatively. "If it gives her pleasure she can take it home, and even if she wanted to carry off kittens or tortoises there would be no call to get worked up about it, Fräulein Rottenmeier."

Heidi hastily gathered up her bundle, her eyes gleaming with happiness and gratitude. When they reached the carriage Herr Sesemann took her hand and said in a friendly voice that he and Klara would often think of her and that he wished her a smooth journey. Heidi thanked him warmly for the many kindnesses she had received. "And please give Dr Classen a thousand thanks and greetings from me," she added. She had not forgotten that yesterday the doctor had said all would be well in the morning. Now all was well, and Heidi thought he must have helped make it so.

She was lifted into the carriage, and the basket, a travel hamper and Sebastian went in after her. Herr Sesemann called out one last cheery goodbye and they moved off.

Shortly afterwards Heidi was sitting in a railway carriage, her hands clasped round the basket on her lap. She would not let go of it for an instant, as it contained the precious bread rolls for Grandmother, which she brooded over carefully and peeped at now and again with great satisfaction. For several hours she sat in silence as it dawned on her for the first time properly that she was on her way home to Grandfather, to the mountains and to Grandmother and Peter. Everything she would see there appeared vividly before her eyes, but as one set of images succeeded another some of her recent fears returned to upset her.

"Sebastian," she blurted out, "are you sure that Grandmother in the mountains hasn't died?"

"Let's hope not. She'll be alive all right," he reassured her.

Heidi fell back into her daydreaming, occasionally looking into the basket. She could hardly wait to set out all the rolls on the table for Grandmother. After a while she spoke again: "Sebastian, if only we could be really certain that Grandmother is still alive."

"Oh, I think we can," replied her half-asleep companion. "She'll be alive. Why shouldn't she be?"

Presently Heidi felt heavy-lidded too, and after her unsettled night and early start she was so tired that she slept soundly until Sebastian gave her arm a good shake and shouted in her ear, "Wake up, wake up! We're in Basel. We must get out!"

Next morning they continued by rail for many more hours. Again Heidi sat with her basket on her lap, firmly resolved not to hand it over to Sebastian. On this day she said nothing at all, and with each passing hour she grew more excited. Then, just when she least expected it, she heard a cry of "Maienfeld". She sprang up from her seat, as did Sebastian, who had also been taken by surprise. A minute later they were standing on the platform with Heidi's trunk while the train puffed on into the valley. Sebastian's eyes followed it wistfully; he would far rather have gone on in the security and ease of a railway carriage than make a long trudge on foot that was bound to end with an uphill climb that could be perilous as well as arduous in this half-wild country – as he assumed it to be.

He looked round warily, wondering whom he could ask about the safest way to the village. Not far from the station was a scrawny horse harnessed to a cart, into which a broad-shouldered man was loading a couple of heavy sacks that had come off the train. Sebastian went up to him and posed his question about the safest way to the village. "There aren't any unsafe ones," came the curt reply.

Sebastian tried again, this time asking about the best way to take without risk of falling into a ravine, and also how a trunk might be conveyed separately. The other man turned to the trunk and scanned it with his eyes for a moment. Then he said he was going to the village himself and would take it on his cart as long as it was not too heavy. After further negotiation it was agreed that the man would take the girl and her trunk, and that someone from the village would be found to escort her up the mountain later that day.

"I know the way from the village, so I can go alone," Heidi interjected, having attended closely to what the two men were saying. Sebastian felt a huge sense of relief at having his apprehensions of an Alpine ascent removed. He discreetly ushered Heidi to one side and gave her a thick roll of banknotes and the letter for Grandfather, explaining that the money was a present from Herr Sesemann which she must put right at the bottom of the basket, under the bread, and be most careful of, because if she lost it Herr Sesemann would be furious and never forgive her.

"Remember what I've said, little miss," he concluded.

"Don't worry, I won't lose it," Heidi assured him, pushing the money and the letter to the bottom of the basket. The

man loaded up the trunk, and then Sebastian lifted Heidi
with her basket onto the seat behind the horse. He shook
her hand to say goodbye and warned her again with various
looks and gestures to keep her eyes on the basket and its
contents, trying to do so inconspicuously since the other man
was close by and knowing that he really ought to have taken
the girl all the way home himself. The man swung himself
up onto the seat beside Heidi and the cart rolled off towards
the higher ground, while Sebastian, glad to have escaped the
fearful prospect of a mountain trek, sat down outside the
little station house and waited for the train to return.

The driver of the cart was the village baker, and the
sacks he was taking home contained flour. He had never
previously seen Heidi, but he had known her parents and,
like everyone in the village, he was familiar with the story
of the girl who had been taken to the Alp Uncle. He soon
surmised that this much discussed person was now sitting
next to him. He was a little surprised, though, to see her
come home so soon, and during the ride he drew her into
a conversation.

"You must be the girl who used to live up with the Alp
Uncle, your grandfather."

"Yes."

"You must have had a bad time of it to be making the
long journey home again so soon."

"Not at all. No one could live better than people do in
Frankfurt."

"So why are you running home?"

"Because Herr Sesemann said I could. Otherwise I
wouldn't have done it."

"Bah, but why didn't you just stay there, even if you were allowed to leave?

"Because I'm a thousand times happier with Grandfather on the mountainside than anywhere in the world."

"You'll think differently when you get back up there," the baker muttered. "I can't help wondering, though," he mused to himself. "She must know how it is."

He began to whistle and said nothing more. Heidi looked around and trembled inwardly with emotion as she recognized the trees lining their route and the lofty jagged peaks of the Falknis that seemed to gaze across and greet her like dear old friends. Heidi returned the greeting, and with every rotation of the wheels she became more nervous with excitement, scarcely able to resist jumping down from the cart and running as fast as she could all the way home. Nonetheless she remained seated, quivering all over but not moving.

As they entered the village the clock struck five. In no time a group of women and children was gathered round them, soon joined by a few men from nearby houses, all drawn by the sight of the girl and the trunk on the baker's cart, and wanting to know who she was, where she had come from and where she was going. The baker lifted Heidi down. "Thank you. Grandfather will come for the trunk," she said hastily and wanted to take to her heels, but the way was blocked on every side, and a host of voices asked her all sorts of questions at once. Heidi pressed through the crowd with so much fear etched on her face that people instinctively stepped back to let her pass.

"Did you see how frightened she was? Well, who can blame her?" they murmured. And they reminded one another how in the last year the Alp Uncle had got far worse even than before, never uttering a word to anyone and walking by those who crossed his path with a face like thunder as though he wanted to kill them. If only the girl had some other place in the world to go, she would never rush back up to that dragon's lair. At this point the baker broke in and said he might well know more than any of them. Then he related in the strictest confidence that a gentleman had brought her as far as Maienfeld and parted with her in a very friendly way, paying him what he had demanded to transport her without haggling and even adding a tip. The girl had without doubt been perfectly well where she was, he continued, and was returning to her grandfather of her own free will. This report astounded his audience and spread so rapidly that there was not a house in the village in which the topic of Heidi forsaking a life of comfort to go back to her grandfather was not talked over that same evening.

Heidi sped out of the village as quickly as she could, but now and again she came to an abrupt halt to catch her breath. Her basket was quite heavy, and the higher she climbed the steeper the path became. Heidi had only one thought in her head: "Will Grandmother still be sitting at her place in the corner by her spinning wheel, or will she have died by now?" When she caught sight of the cottage ahead of her in its pastureland hollow her heart leapt, and it beat louder and faster as she broke into a run. In no time she covered the distance. She was shaking so much that she could barely manage the door, but she got it open and rushed into the middle of the little parlour. There she stood, panting hard and unable to speak.

"Good Lord," came a voice from the corner, "that's how our Heidi used to burst in! Oh, if only I could have her here one more time in my life. Who is it that's come in?"

"It's me, Grandmother, it's me!" cried Heidi. She rushed over to the old woman and knelt down, seized hold of her hands and one arm and pressed herself against her. She was too happy to say another word.

At first Grandmother was so taken aback that she too was speechless. Then she put out her hand and stroked Heidi's curly hair, and said again and again, "Yes, this is her hair, and it's her voice too! Oh, God in Heaven, what a gift you have given me today!" A few large, happy tears fell from her blind eyes onto the girl's hand. "Can it be you, Heidi? Have you really come back?"

"Yes, I really have, Grandmother," replied Heidi, eager to convince her. "Don't cry. I'm definitely here, and I'll come to see you every day and never go away again. And look at this, Grandmother, you won't have to eat any hard bread for a while. Just look!" And Heidi took the rolls from her basket one by one and piled up all twelve on Grandmother's lap.

"Ah, dear child! What a blessing you have brought me!" exclaimed Grandmother, as roll after roll appeared and the pile kept getting bigger. "But the greatest blessing is yourself, my dear!" She reached again for Heidi's hair and caressed her hot cheeks: "Say something else, my dear, anything, just so I can hear your voice."

So Heidi told Grandmother how dreadfully afraid she had been that she might not find her alive, and that she would never be able to visit her again or give her the white rolls.

Just then Peter's mother came in, and for a second she stopped short in astonishment. "It's Heidi, to be sure, but how can that be?" she cried.

Heidi got to her feet and shook hands with her. Brigitte could not get over her appearance, and she went right round her to take it all in. "Grandmother," she said, "if only you could see what a pretty frock Heidi has and how she looks. I barely recognized her. And the little hat with a feather on the table is yours too, I suppose. Put it on quickly so I can see how it suits you."

"No, I don't want to," said Heidi firmly. "You can have it. I don't need it any more – I've got my own."

So saying, she undid her red bundle and drew out her old hat, which was more misshapen than ever after the journey. But that did not worry Heidi, who remembered Grandfather's parting words that he never wanted to see her with a feather in her hat. Indeed, it was the constant thought of going home to Grandfather that had made her preserve her old hat so carefully. Brigitte told her not to be such a simpleton as to give away her splendid new one. She couldn't accept it, she said, but if Heidi didn't want it maybe she could sell it to the village schoolmaster's daughter for a good price. Heidi was not to be persuaded, however, and she placed the hat discreetly out of sight behind Grandmother's seat in the corner. Then she removed her frock and, standing in her petticoat with bare arms, wrapped the red scarf around herself. Having done so, she held the old woman's hand and said, "Now I must go to Grandfather, but I'll come again tomorrow. Goodnight, Grandmother!"

"Yes, do come again, Heidi! Come again tomorrow!" Grandmother urged her, pressing her hand and reluctant to let her go.

"Why have you taken off your pretty frock?" asked Brigitte.

"I'd sooner go to Grandfather like this; otherwise he might not know me. You hardly knew me in it."

Brigitte accompanied Heidi outside and spoke to her in a slightly mysterious tone: "You could have kept the frock on, you know. He would have known you all right. But you should be careful in other ways. Our Peter says the Alp Uncle is always in a black mood now and never says a word."

Heidi said goodnight and continued up the mountain with her basket under her arm. The evening sun lit up the green pastureland all around, and farther away the gleaming surface of the great Schesaplana snowfield came into view. Heidi could not resist stopping and looking back every few steps, for the highest peaks were behind her. A minute later a red shimmer falling over the grass before her climbing feet made her turn round again, and there – more magnificent than she had recalled or even beheld in her dreams – were the rocky horns of the Falknis, searing like flames into the sky, while the snowfield glowed and rose-pink clouds scudded by. The grass all over the pasture was gilded, glittering rock faces shone down, and the entire valley below was bathed in a golden perfume.

Heidi stood amid this splendour with bright tears of joy running down her cheeks, and in her bliss she clasped her hands and looked up to Heaven. In a strong, clear voice she thanked the Lord that He had brought her back home and that everything around her was still so beautiful, much more so than she had remembered, and that it was all hers again. She felt so happy, so enriched by the glorious scenery that she wished she could find more words of thanks for God.

Not until the light began to fade was Heidi ready to move on. Now she ran up the mountainside, and before long she could make out the tips of the fir trees above the roof of Grandfather's cottage, then the roof itself and the whole cottage. Grandfather was sitting on the bench against the front wall smoking his pipe, and behind his home the crowns of the trees swayed in the evening breeze. Heidi started running faster, and before the Alp Uncle could see who or what was approaching she raced up to him, threw her basket to the ground and flung her arms round him. In her emotion at being reunited with him she could only repeat a single word: "Grandfather! Grandfather! Grandfather!"

The old man was struck dumb. For the first time in years his eyes filled with tears, and he had to wipe them away with his hand. Then he loosened Heidi's arms from his neck, set her on his knee and had a good look at her. "You've come home, then, Heidi!" he said at last. "How so? You don't look overly grand. Did they send you away?"

"Oh no, Grandfather," she replied eagerly, "you mustn't think that. They were all very kind, Klara and Grandmamma and Herr Sesemann. But you see, Grandfather, I longed to be back home with you. It was unbearable, and sometimes it suffocated me so much I thought I might choke. I didn't say anything, though, because that would have been ungrateful. And then out of the blue Herr Sesemann asked to see me very early one morning – but I think it was Dr Classen's doing – but maybe it's all in the letter."

Heidi quickly dropped to the ground, took the letter and the roll of banknotes from the basket and handed both to Grandfather.

"This belongs to you," he said, placing the money to one side on the bench. The letter he opened and read through, and then without a word he slipped it into his pocket.

"Would you perhaps like to drink some milk with me again, Heidi?" he asked, taking her by the hand to lead her into the cottage. "But keep your money with you. You could buy a whole bed with it and enough clothes to last a couple of years."

"I don't need it, Grandfather," Heidi declared. "I already have a bed, and Klara packed so many clothes for me I'm sure I'll never want any more."

"Bring it anyway and put it in the cupboard. One day it will come in useful."

Heidi did as Grandfather said and skipped into the cottage after him. In her pleasure at seeing her old home she darted into every corner and up the ladder – but at the top she came to a sudden halt and called down in bewilderment, "But Grandfather, my bed's gone!"

"It will be there again soon," he replied from below. "I didn't know you would be back. Now come and have your milk!"

Heidi went down and sat on her tall chair in its old spot. She raised her bowl and drank with great relish, as if nothing so fine had ever passed her lips, and after a big intake of breath she put the bowl down and said, "Nothing in the world tastes as good as our milk, Grandfather."

Just then they heard a piercing whistle outside, and Heidi shot like lightning through the door. Hopping, skipping and jumping down the mountain came the whole herd of goats, with Peter in their midst. When he spotted Heidi he stopped as if rooted to the spot and stared at her mutely. Shouting "Hello, Peter", she rushed forward into the herd. "Cygnet, Little Bear, do you still recognize me?" The little creatures must have known her voice at once, for they rubbed their heads against her and began bleating vigorously for joy. Heidi greeted all the goats by name, and they gambolled around in a mad tangle and pressed towards her. The impatient Thistle Finch leapt up in the air, clearing two other goats to reach her more quickly, and even the timid Snow Hop stubbornly rammed the mighty Turk aside, leaving him standing in amazement at her impudence and waving his beard aloft to make his presence felt.

Heidi was beside herself with pleasure at being with her old companions again. She kept embracing the delicate little Snow Hop and stroked the tempestuous Thistle Finch. In their frenzy to display their trust and love for her, the goats pushed and shoved her to and fro, until at last she came close to where Peter still stood motionless.

"Come here, Peter, and say hello properly!" Heidi called up to him, holding out her hand.

"So you're back, then," said the startled boy, finally finding his voice, and he came over and took her extended hand. Then he asked the question he had always asked at the end of their days together on the pastureland: "Will you come again tomorrow?"

"No, not tomorrow, but maybe the day after. Tomorrow I'm going to Grandmother."

"It's good that you're back," said Peter, contorting his face into an expression of immense glee. Then he prepared to continue his descent, but he had more trouble with his goats than ever before. Even when his coaxing and threats had at last succeeded in gathering the animals about him, the sight of Heidi walking away with one arm round Cygnet and the other round Little Bear made them all break loose and run after her. She had to go into the pen with her two goats and shut the door; otherwise Peter would never have been able to set off with his herd.

When Heidi went inside the cottage she saw that her bed had been made up again. It was impressively high and sweet-smelling, for the hay had only just been got in, and Grandfather had carefully spread clean linen sheets over it. Heidi felt a thrill as she lay down on the bed, and she slept more soundly than she had for an entire year. During the night Grandfather must have got up ten times and climbed the ladder with his ears pricked to make sure she was asleep and not restless. He also checked that the hay he had stuffed into the skylight to prevent the moonlight coming in and shining on her bed was still in place. There was no need to worry: Heidi slept without interruption and did not budge from where she lay. Her great, burning desire had been satisfied. She had seen all the peaks and rock faces in the sunset, and she had heard the rustling of the firs. She was back in her Alpine home.

Chapter 14

Church Bells on Sunday

HEIDI STOOD UNDER the swaying firs and waited for Grandfather, who was going to walk to the village to fetch the trunk while she visited Grandmother. She looked forward intensely to seeing Grandmother again and hearing how she had liked the bread rolls, yet she was in no hurry because she could not get enough of the old familiar rustling of the trees above her and the sparkle and scent of the green pastures with their golden flowers.

Grandfather came out of the cottage, glanced around and said contentedly, "Good, let's be off." It was a Saturday, and it was his habit on this day to tidy up and clean everything in the house, the goat pen and the other outside areas. Today he had given over the morning to this task so he could go out with Heidi in the early afternoon, and everything now looked as he wished.

CHAPTER 14

They parted ways at the goatherd's cottage and Heidi bounded in. Grandmother had already heard her footfall and called out affectionately, "Are you there, my dear? Have you come again?" And she took Heidi's hand and held it tight, still fearing that the child could be snatched away from her again. Their first subject was the bread rolls, and Grandmother said they tasted just delicious and had done her a power of good. Peter's mother added that Grandmother had been so concerned about getting through them too quickly that she had only eaten one since yesterday, but that eating one each day for a week would certainly make her much stronger. Heidi paid close attention to Brigitte's words and fell into contemplation for a few moments. Then an idea came to her.

"I know what I'll do, Grandmother," she exclaimed happily. "I'll write to Klara, and I'm sure she'll send me as many rolls as we have now, or maybe twice as many, because I had a whole heap exactly like these in my wardrobe, and when they were taken away Klara said she would give me just as many again, and she's sure to do it."

"Goodness me," said Brigitte, "that's a nice thought, but remember they'll go stale in getting here. If only I had a few pennies to spare now and again. The baker in the village makes rolls like that too, but I can barely afford the brown ones."

A ray of ecstasy shone across Heidi's face. "Oh Grandmother, I have no end of money," she cried jubilantly and jumped up and down, "and now I know what I'll do with it! You must have a fresh white roll every day,

175

and two on Sunday, and Peter can bring them from the village."

"No, no, my dear," Grandmother replied. "That cannot be. The money wasn't given to you for that. You must let your grandfather have it and he'll tell you what to do with it."

But Heidi's high spirits were not to be dampened. She rejoiced and frisked round the room, chanting, "Now Grandmother can have a bread roll every day and she'll get strong again." And then, more exultantly: "Oh, Grandmother, if you get quite healthy your sight will come back too! Maybe you only lost it because you were so weak."

The old woman said nothing, not wishing to deflate her. As Heidi was skipping about she suddenly caught sight of Grandmother's old prayer book, and this gave her another happy idea: "Grandmother, I can read very well now. Shall I read out a hymn from your book?"

"Oh, yes!" replied Grandmother, marvelling at what she heard. "But can you really, my dear, can you really read?"

Heidi climbed onto a chair and took down the book, which had lain so long untouched that it released a thick cloud of dust. She wiped it clean, sat on her stool beside Grandmother and asked what she should read.

"Whatever you like, my dear." And the old woman, having pushed her spinning wheel aside, waited on the edge of her seat.

Heidi leafed through the book, murmuring a line here and there to herself. "Here's one about the sun, Grandmother. I'll read you that." She began quietly, but slowly her voice grew warm and keen:

"In golden resplendence
The sun casts its light,
With blissful abundance
Our hearts to delight,
Bathing the world in its bountiful rays.

"My head was bowed,
My limbs were aching;
But now I stand proud,
Glad tidings awaiting,
And turn unto Heaven my marvelling gaze.

"My eyes behold
God's shaping hand.
His glories unfold
And I understand
That truly His power is boundless.

"If men live in charity
And worship the Lord
And die full of piety,
They gain their reward,
For their spirit shall dwell in His fastness.

"Earthly things perish,
But God endures still.
Nothing can vanquish
His Word or His will,
Which spring from immutable ground.

"His merciful balm
Can soothe our distress,
Shield us from harm,
Make sorrows hurt less,
All pain now and ever confound.

"Life's woe and unease
Expire like the night,
And stormy high seas
Grow calm in the light
Of the sun, and our yearning is stilled.

"And now I may rest
In fields of enchantment,
Abode of the blest,
In tranquil contentment,
My mind's sweetest vision – fulfilled."

Grandmother sat still, her hands folded, and despite the tears running down her cheeks her face wore an expression of unutterable bliss such as Heidi had never before seen in her. When she had finished, the old woman pleaded, "Read it again, Heidi, let me hear it one more time."

"Life's woe and unease
Expire like the night."

And the girl repeated the last two verses with heartfelt joy:

"Life's woe and unease
Expire like the night,
And stormy high seas
Grow calm in the light
Of the sun, and our yearning is stilled.

"And now I may rest
In fields of enchantment,
Abode of the blest,
In tranquil contentment,
My mind's sweetest vision – fulfilled."

"Oh, Heidi, how clear it is, like a light to the heart! What a comfort you have given me!"

Again and again Grandmother spoke of her joy, and Heidi kept her eyes fixed on her and beamed with pleasure too, for she had never seen her like this. Gone was the old doleful face, and instead she looked happy and grateful, as if she already had those beautiful fields of enchantment before her and new eyes to see them with.

There was a knock at the window, and Heidi saw Grandfather outside beckoning her home. She left straight away, having assured Grandmother that she would return the next day, and that even if she went out with Peter to graze the goats she would still come in the afternoon. The idea that she could make Grandmother cheerful again and bring light to her life was the greatest felicity Heidi had ever known, greater still, and by far, than being with the goats among the flowers of the sunlit pastureland.

Brigitte ran out after her with the frock and hat, which were still in the cottage. Heidi draped the frock over her arm, reflecting that the risk of Grandfather not recognizing her was gone, but the hat she rejected outright. She would never ever wear it, she said, and Brigitte should keep it.

Heidi's heart was so elated by what had passed that she lost no time in telling Grandfather her news: that white rolls for Grandmother could be got from the village as long as there was money to pay for them, and that Grandmother had seen a new light and felt its comfort. Once Heidi had finished the second topic she went back to the first. "Grandfather," she said in a confiding tone, "I know Grandmother is against it, but will you give me the money so I can give Peter enough for a roll each day and two on Sunday?"

"What about the bed, Heidi?" he replied. "It would be good for you to have a proper bed, and there would still be enough for some rolls."

But Heidi gave him no peace, insisting she slept far better on her bed of hay than she ever had on her soft mattress in Frankfurt. She urged him so relentlessly that at last he said, "The money is yours, so do as you wish with it. If you spend it on bread for Grandmother you can supply her for many a long year."

Heidi rejoiced: "Hurray! Now she'll never have to eat any more hard brown bread, and – oh Grandfather – now everything is better then ever before in our whole lives!"

She jumped up high while holding Grandfather's hand, sporting like the merriest bird in the sky. Then, all at once, she grew serious and said, "You know, if God had answered my prayer straight away none of this would have happened. I would have come home quickly and only brought Grandmother a few rolls, and I wouldn't have been able to read to her, which does her good. But God thought of everything and made it much better than I could have imagined. It has all come about as Grandmamma said. Oh, how happy I am that God didn't yield despite my pleading and despair! But now I will always pray and give thanks to the Lord, as Grandmamma said I should, and if He doesn't answer my prayer I'll know He has something better in mind, just like in Frankfurt. So let's say our prayers every day, Grandfather, and never forget, so that God doesn't forget us."

"And what if someone does forget?" asked Grandfather in a faltering voice.

"He'll be badly off, because the Lord will forget him and let him fend for himself, and if he ever gets into trouble and bewails his fate no one will pity him, and everyone will say: he forsook God, and now God, who could help, forsakes him."

"That's so true, Heidi! How do you know all this?"

"Grandmamma explained it to me."

The old man walked on in silence. Then, picking up his train of thought, he muttered, "So be it. When God has forsaken someone he must accept his fate. There's no turning back."

"Oh no, Grandfather, he can turn back! Grandmamma told me that too, and then it turns out like the beautiful story in my book. You don't know it, but soon we'll be home and you'll see how beautiful the story is."

In her impatience, Heidi walked faster and faster up the final stretch of the slope, and as they neared the cottage she let go of his hand and dashed inside. Grandfather swung a basket with some of Heidi's things off his back – the trunk had been too heavy for him to carry up, so he had put half of its contents into the basket – and sat down pensively on the bench. Heidi ran back to him with the big book under her arm. "That's good – you're already sitting down," she said, making one final leap to his side and turning to the story, which she had read so many countless times that the pages naturally fell open at the right place. She began to read with fervour the story of the young man who had a good life at home, wearing a rich coat and standing among the fine cattle and sheep that grazed his father's fields, leaning on his staff and watching the sunset, exactly as he appeared in the picture.

"But one day he decided he wanted to be his own master and have his own possessions. He demanded his share from his father, went out into the world and squandered it. When all his money was gone he was forced to take work as a farm labourer. Rather than the fine animals in his father's fields, the farmer had only pigs, which it was the young man's job to look after. He had nothing but rags to cover his body and small portions of the spent grain for the pigs to eat. When he thought of the life he had left behind, the kindness he had received from his father and his own ungrateful conduct, he shed tears of homesickness and remorse. He resolved to go to his father and beg his forgiveness, and say to him, 'I am no longer worthy to be called your son, but let me be a hand on your farm!'

"As he was approaching his old home, still some distance away, his father saw him and rushed out... And what do you think happens next, Grandfather?" asked Heidi, looking up from the page. "Do you think the father will still be angry and say, 'I told you so!'? Well, just listen to what comes now. When his father saw him he was filled with pity. He ran to meet him and embraced and kissed him, and his son said, 'Father, I have sinned against you and against Heaven, and I am no longer worthy to be called your son.' But the father said to his labourers, 'Bring me the best robe for him to wear and give him a ring for his finger and shoes for his feet, and fetch the fatted calf to be killed so that we can eat and be merry, for my son that was dead is now alive; he was lost and now is found.' And they feasted together."

Heidi expected Grandfather to like and admire the story, so when he sat still and said nothing she said, "It's a beautiful story, isn't it, Grandfather?"

"Yes, Heidi, it certainly is," he replied, but his features were so grave that she fell silent and studied the pictures in her book. Then she gently slid it in front of him and pointed at the picture of the returning prodigal standing in his new robe next to his father, once more belonging to him as his son. "Look how happy he is," she said.

Some hours later, when Heidi was fast asleep, Grandfather went up the ladder and put his lamp down by her bed so that the light fell upon her. She had not forgotten to say her prayers, and her hands were still folded. Her rosy little face bore an expression of peace and blessed trust that must have touched the old man, for he stood there without moving for many minutes, his eyes riveted on the sleeping child. Then he folded his hands too and bowed his head, and in a low voice he said, "Father, I have sinned against you and against Heaven, and I am no longer worthy to be called your son." And two large tears rolled down his cheeks.

In a few hours more, not long after daybreak, the Alp Uncle stood in front of his cottage and looked around keenly. The Sunday morning light sparkled across the mountains and valleys. A few matins bells could be heard from below, and in the fir trees the birds sang their dawn melodies. He stepped back into the cottage and called up to the loft, "Come on, Heidi, the sun is up! Put your best frock on and we'll go to church together!"

Heidi did not tarry. This was quite a new summons from him, one to follow with all speed. In no time she got into her pretty Frankfurt dress and shot down the ladder, but when she saw him she stopped short and stared in amazement. "Oh, Grandfather, I've never seen you like this before," she blurted out at last. "It's the first time you've worn the coat with silver buttons! You look so nice in your Sunday best!"

The old man smiled at her contentedly: "And you look nice in yours! Well, come along." He took Heidi's hand and they set off down the mountain together.

Now the bells rang out cheerily from all sides, and the sound grew richer and fuller the further they went. Heidi listened with delight. "Can you hear, Grandfather? It's like one great big celebration."

Everyone was already in the village church singing the first hymn when Grandfather and Heidi came in and sat in the back pew. Before the hymn was finished, the man sitting nearest to them nudged his neighbour on the other side and said, "Did you see that? The Alp Uncle here in church!" His neighbour nudged the next person and so on, and in no time whispers spread all through the congregation: "The Alp Uncle! The Alp Uncle!" Few of the women could resist a quick peep over their shoulders, causing most to lose their place in the hymn and making it difficult for the cantor to keep the voices in unison. But when the pastor began his sermon everyone listened attentively, because the warm praise and thanksgiving in his words spoke to their hearts and filled them with joy.

At the end of the service the Alp Uncle left the church holding Heidi's hand and walked over to the pastor's house. All those who came out with him or were already standing outside looked after him, and most followed to see if he really would enter the house, which he did. Then they gathered in little groups and chattered excitedly about his unprecedented appearance in church. They looked eagerly at the parson's door, wondering how the Alp Uncle would emerge, whether angry after a quarrel with the pastor or in harmony with him, for they had no idea what had brought the old man down and what he had in mind.

Despite everything a new sentiment was springing up in many of them. "Perhaps the Alp Uncle is not as black as he's painted," said one man to another. "You saw how protectively he held the girl's hand."

"It's what I've always said," came the reply, "and if he was all bad he wouldn't go to see the pastor. It would give him the jitters. Anyway, people always exaggerate."

And the baker said, "Wasn't I the first to tell you? Who ever heard of a little girl with as much to eat and drink as she likes, and everything else she could want, and then giving it all up to go and live with a grandfather who's so horrible and bad-tempered that she has to be scared of him?"

Bit by bit a mood of affectionate regard took hold of the crowd, the more so as the men were presently joined by the women, who had heard various things from Peter's mother and grandmother that contradicted the general view of the Alp Uncle and now suddenly seemed quite credible. As the minutes went by they all felt increasingly as if they were waiting to welcome an old and long-missed friend.

Meanwhile, the Alp Uncle had reached the pastor's study and knocked on the door. The pastor opened it and stepped towards his visitor, not with the surprise he might have shown, rather as if he had been expecting him. He must have noticed the old man's unaccustomed presence in church, and now he grasped his hand and pumped it heartily. For a moment the Alp Uncle, who was not prepared for such a cordial reception, was at a loss to know what to say. Then he collected himself:

"I've come to ask you to forget the words I spoke when you called on me, and not to bear me any rancour for setting my face against your well-meant advice. You were right in everything you said, and I was wrong, but now I'm willing to do as you proposed and take up winter quarters in the village. Conditions higher up are too harsh for the girl in the colder months. And if the villagers look askance at me and think I'm not to be trusted it's my own fault, and I'm sure you won't treat me that way."

The pastor's kindly eyes gleamed with pleasure, and he took the old man's hand in his and shook it again. With emotion in his voice he said, "Neighbour, your spirit was in the best church of all before your body came to mine. How glad I am! You won't regret your decision to come down and live among us. In my home you'll always be welcome as a dear friend and neighbour, and I hope that during the long winter evenings we'll pass many a pleasant hour together. I very much look forward to your company, and we'll find some nice friends for the little one too."

As the pastor spoke, he gently patted the top of Heidi's curly head, and then took her hand as he accompanied them both to the front door. He walked out of the house with them before saying goodbye, and all the people standing around saw him shake the Alp Uncle's hand several times, as if he were parting reluctantly with his closest friend.

No sooner had the pastor gone back inside and shut the door than the whole crowd surged towards the Alp Uncle. Everybody wanted to get to him first, and so many hands were simultaneously thrust at him that he did not know which to take first. "What a pleasure it is, a real pleasure, to have you among us again!" one person called out. "I've been meaning to talk to you for ages, Alp Uncle!" exclaimed another. On and on they came, pressing forward in a body to speak to him. He responded to their cordial greetings by telling them he intended to move back to the village for the winter and mix with his old acquaintances. This raised an even greater clamour, and an observer would have concluded that he was the most popular figure in the community and that they had felt his absence keenly.

Most of them escorted the Alp Uncle and Heidi the best part of the way back to their cottage, and on saying good-bye he had to assure them all that he would call on them when he next came to the village. As they walked back down the mountain the old man stood still and followed them with his eyes, his face suffused with a warm glow as if the sun were shining from within him. Heidi gazed up at him and said delightedly, "Grandfather, you look more and more handsome today. I've never seen you like this."

"Do I indeed?" he laughed. "Well, Heidi, you see, today I'm happy beyond my deserts and comprehension. To be at peace with God and man is a wonderful feeling! The Lord meant well by me when he sent you up the mountain."

When they reached the goatherd's cottage, Grandfather opened the door and went straight in. "Good day, Grandmother," he called out. "I think we'd better make some more repairs before the autumn winds come."

"Heavens above, it's the Alp Uncle!" cried Grandmother in joyful surprise. "Of all the unexpected things! I'm so glad I can thank you once more for everything you did for us. God bless you! God bless you!"

Trembling with happiness, the old woman held out her hand, which he shook warmly. Then she continued, still holding his hand, "And I also have something to ask of you, Alp Uncle, something close to my heart. If ever I've wronged you please don't punish me by letting Heidi go away again before I'm in my grave by the church. You don't know what she means to me!" And she clasped the girl, who had already huddled up to her, even tighter.

"Don't worry, Grandmother," he reassured her. "I won't punish you or myself by doing that. We'll all stay together now, and for a long time yet, God willing."

Then Brigitte, drawing the Alp Uncle furtively into the corner, showed him the hat with a feather and explained how it came to be there. She could not deprive a child of such a possession, she said.

But he looked across at his Heidi approvingly and said, "It's her hat, but I don't blame her for not wanting to wear it, and if she'd like you to have it then take it!"

Brigitte was overjoyed at this unexpected decision. "It must be worth more than ten francs. Just look at it!" And she gleefully put the hat on her head. "What a boon going to Frankfurt has been to Heidi! I've been wondering if I ought to send Peter there for a while too. What do you think, Alp Uncle?"

His eyes danced merrily, and he said he thought it could do Peter no harm, but she ought to wait for the right opportunity to present itself.

Just then Peter himself charged through the door, having run his head into it so hard that everything in the house rattled. He had come in great haste and stood panting heavily in the middle of the room with a letter in his outstretched hand. Being handed a letter in the village post office had been a quite novel experience for him. It was addressed to Heidi, and they all sat round the table with baited breath as she opened it and, without prompting, began reading aloud.

The letter was from Klara Sesemann. She wrote that life in the house had been so dull since Heidi's departure that she did not know how much longer she could stand it, and that in response to her constant pleading her father had decided that they would travel to Bad Ragaz in the autumn. Grandmamma would come too, as she wished to visit Heidi and Grandfather in their Alpine home. Grandmamma also wanted Heidi to know that she had been right to take the bread rolls for Grandmother; that there was some coffee on its way so she did not have to eat them dry; and that when she came herself Heidi should take her to see Grandmother.

This news was such a happy surprise, and gave them so much to say and so many questions to ask about a prospect they all looked forward to greatly, that even Grandfather did not notice how late it was getting. The thought of the days ahead and, perhaps even more, the pleasure of being together that very afternoon made them all thoroughly contented and cheerful.

"There's nothing like an old friend coming back after many years and giving you his hand," Grandmother said at last. "It brings comfort to my heart and makes me think that one day I'll be reunited with all those who were dear to me. You'll come again soon, Alp Uncle, won't you? And Heidi tomorrow?"

This they solemnly promised her, and then it was time to say goodbye. Grandfather and Heidi made their way back up the mountain, and just as the clear peal of bells near and far had called them down in the morning, so now the gentle sound of the vespers rose from the valley and accompanied them back to their cottage, which shimmered on their approach in the Sunday evening light.

And when Grandmamma comes to visit in the autumn there will no doubt be many more happy surprises for Heidi and for Grandmother, and in no time a proper bed will be installed in the hayloft. For Grandmamma brings order to people's lives wherever she is – and peace to their hearts.

EXTRA MATERIAL
FOR YOUNG READERS

THE WRITER

Johanna Spyri was born on 12th June 1827 in Hirzel, a rural area outside Zurich. Although she is one of the world's best-loved children's writers, little is known of her life. Her childhood was spent in the small and quiet village of Hirzel, where she had beautiful views of the surrounding mountains. Hers was a happy and comfortable home, and Johanna, along with her five siblings, grew up surrounded by music and books. The little village in which much of *Heidi* is set was not based on Hirzel, however, but another part of Switzerland entirely. Maienfeld, the town near Grandfather's house in the book, is a real place, just as the flame-red Falknis and mighty Schesaplana are both mountains in the Rätikon range. This area of Switzerland was the beloved location in which Johanna spent many happy family holidays.

Johanna left home after getting married at the age of twenty-five, and she gave much of her time to charities and helping others. She loved travelling, music, art and books, yet she also described her "inner life" as being "full of storms". One reason, perhaps, for this turmoil was her temporary loss of faith. Moreover, while she lived for most of her adult life in the city of Zurich, Johanna sometimes found city life oppressive and difficult.

Her husband and child sadly passed away in 1884, and Johanna devoted herself in her remaining years to charitable causes and her writing. She died in 1901 in Zurich. She remains a national treasure in Switzerland, even featuring on a postage stamp in 1951 and a coin in 2009.

THE BOOK

Johanna adored reading, yet she didn't have her first book published until she was over forty years old. Much of her early writing was for adult readers, and was well received, but *Heidi*, published in two parts in 1880 (*Heidi: Lessons at Home and Abroad*, the text contained in this volume) and 1881 (*Heidi: Putting Her Lessons to Good Use*) – when Johanna was over fifty – was a spectacular success. The book, written in German, was swiftly translated into English and achieved fame around the world, becoming one of the best-selling children's books ever written. Today, of all Johanna's books, *Heidi* is the only one that remains well known. Its sequels, *Heidi Grows Up* and *Heidi's Children*, were written by her first English translator, Charles Tritten.

More than twenty film and television adaptations of *Heidi* have been produced, and the book even gave rise to the tourist area known as Heidiland in eastern Switzerland, in tribute to Johanna's much loved book.

THE CHARACTERS

Heidi
Adelheid, known by almost everyone as Heidi, is around five years old at the beginning of the novel. She is kind, compassionate and free-spirited, always thinking of ways to help others. She cares deeply about those who suffer, both humans and animals, and is at her happiest among the mountains, the fir trees and the flowers of her beloved Alpine home.

Alp Uncle (Grandfather)
Known as Grandfather by Heidi and Alp Uncle by everyone else, he is a gruff, grumpy and solitary figure who lives up the mountain away from the other villagers. The townsfolk whisper about his troubled past, but Heidi's presence in his life brings out his true kindness.

Peter
The local goatherd, Peter has a faithful and kind heart, but he is far more interested in a good meal than attending school. He introduces Heidi to the wonders of the mountains and his herd of goats, but he often becomes a little jealous if Heidi spends time with others.

Grandmother

Before she meets Heidi, Peter's blind grandmother is a frail, frightened and melancholy woman. However, the young girl's kindness and lust for life lifts the old lady's spirits. While she is thrown into despair by Heidi moving to Frankfurt, the latter's return and newfound ability to read bring joy once more into the kind old lady's life.

Dete

Dete, Heidi's aunt, looks after the little girl for the first few years of her life. With the offer of employment in Frankfurt, Dete decides to give Heidi to Alp Uncle so that he can look after her. Upon hearing of a comfortable life for a little girl in Frankfurt, she thinks it would offer Heidi the chance of a better future and brings her niece to fill the position. She is unaware, however, of Heidi's love of her mountain home and practically abducts Heidi in taking the child to an unwanted and often unhappy new life in Frankfurt.

Klara Sesemann

Klara is the twelve-year-old daughter of the wealthy Herr Sesemann. Poor Klara is unwell and Heidi is brought to Frankfurt as a companion for her. Klara is brave, extremely generous and thoughtful, and the two girls become firm friends.

Grandmamma

Although she comes to the house with a formidable reputation, Grandmamma, Herr Sesemann's mother and Klara's grandmother, is a warm-hearted and caring lady. She looks after Heidi, helping her learn to read and teaching her about God.

Fräulein Rottenmeier
Fräulein Rottenmeier, Herr Sesemann's housekeeper, is a callous, cold and somewhat cruel lady. She finds fault with everything that Heidi does due to the little girl's unfamiliarity with city life.

Herr Sesemann
A wealthy Frankfurt businessman, he cares deeply about his daughter Klara. He is often away on business, but he tries to ensure that Heidi has a happy life in his house.

Brigitte
Brigitte, Peter's mother, is a quiet and gentle lady. Like Grandmother, she looks forward to Heidi's visits and tells the other villagers of Alp Uncle's kind-heartedness.

Dr Classen
A friend of Herr Sesemann, Dr Classen is a thoughtful and empathetic man. He notices Heidi's homesickness and persuades Herr Sesemann to send her back to her grandfather in the mountains.

Sebastian, Johann and Tinette
The staff in the Sesemann household. Tinette is scornful and unkind; however, Sebastian is a friend

to Heidi while she is in Frankfurt, helping her whenever he can.

Tobias and Adelheid
Heidi's parents, who have sadly passed away.

The Tutor
Employed by Herr Sesemann to teach Klara and Heidi, he is not a very effective teacher and takes an inordinately long time to say anything.

Barbel
A friend of Dete's from Prättigau.

OTHER CLASSIC STORIES
OF ORPHANS

Heidi is the story of an orphan – someone who does not have any parents. Despite her unfortunate situation, Heidi is a happy girl, full of joy and wonder, particularly when amongst nature. She lives with her grandfather, who loves her very much, and she is surrounded by dear friends, from Peter and Grandmother to the goats Snow Hop and Cygnet. While Heidi is rather homesick in Herr Sesemann's house, Klara too becomes a wonderful friend, and the time in Frankfurt brings Heidi many benefits, such as learning to read and finding her faith in God.

There are many classic children's stories about orphans. Setting off from such an unpropitious beginning, the characters invariably display bravery, kindness and an unbreakable spirit. A loving presence, often a family member or foster-parent, comes into their life and offers the support and family they crave. We as readers are drawn into the world of these orphans – from Harry Potter and Oliver Twist to Pippi Longstocking and Anne Shirley – as they are likely to face greater challenges than those who are born and raised in loving families. Here are three other stories of courageous and kind-hearted girls who have to struggle to make the best of their unfortunate starts in life.

Pollyanna

Pollyanna is the title of a novel by Eleanor H. Porter, published in 1913. It is the story of Pollyanna Whittier, an orphan, who is sent to live with her somewhat harsh aunt. Pollyanna, however, has a secret weapon: her father taught her to play the "glad game". Whatever happens to her, and whatever situation she finds herself in, she plays the game and finds something to be truly glad about. Pollyanna's ceaseless optimism and happiness begin to rub off on the community as a whole and even on her aunt. This brings unforeseen love into the lives of two people very dear to Pollyanna and leads the entire town to support her when she is in need. The novel was so successful that soon "Pollyanna" came to mean someone who is extremely cheerful and optimistic. Despite the fact that Pollyanna is a child, her attitude is a lesson to the adults of the town, and she inspires them to be kinder to one another and more grateful for what they have.

Anne of Green Gables

Written by L.M. Montgomery, a Canadian author, and published in 1908, *Anne of Green Gables* tells the heart-warming story of Anne Shirley. Anne is an orphan who is adopted by a brother and sister, Matthew and Marilla Cuthbert, who live at Green Gables, a beautiful farm on Prince Edward Island in Canada. While the siblings had wanted to adopt a boy, Anne's cheerfulness, intelligence and sweet nature swiftly win them round. Anne has a wonderfully vivid imagination and spends her days daydreaming in the woods, fields and lakes of the island. The previously harsh Marilla softens and grows to love Anne dearly, while Matthew happily bends to the child's every whim. She brings an unforeseen happiness and light into the siblings' lives, and despite her extraordinary intelligence opening up new possibilities for her in life, Anne's selflessness – and her love for Green Gables – means that she cannot stand to be away from her loving family.

The Secret Garden

This book was written by Frances Hodgson Burnett, who also wrote the classic *Little Lord Fauntleroy* and *The Little Princess*. *The Secret Garden* tells the tale of ten-year-old Mary Lennox, who after her parents pass away is sent to live with her quiet and unhappy uncle in his remote home in Yorkshire. Unlike Shirley and Pollyanna, Mary is not particularly likeable at the beginning of the novel. She has been neglected by her parents and spoilt by the servants, yet soon the kindness of Martha, the maid, brings out Mary's inner goodness. With her new friends Colin and Dickon, a whole new world of joy both in nature and in being with other people opens up before Mary, and she becomes a happy and optimistic child. This change means that her uncle, long grieving for his deceased wife, is inspired to turn over a new leaf, and he begins to care once more for his son Colin and, of course, for Mary.

TEST YOURSELF

Did you read *Heidi* with the same wonder as the girl herself felt as she climbed the mountain with Peter and the goats and gazed at the beautiful summer flowers? Try this fun quiz to find out, and then turn over for the answers.

1. In Chapter Three, Peter tells Heidi the names of all the goats. What is the name of the goat that has lost its mother, leading Heidi to say that it could come to her if anything was ever the matter?
    A) Snow Hop
    B) Turk
    C) Snow White
    D) Thistle Finch

2. In Chapter Four, a blanket of snow stops Heidi visiting Grandmother for the first time. Eventually, despite the snow, Grandfather agrees to take her. How do they get down the mountain?
    A) On skis
    B) Wearing snowshoes

C) On a sledge

D) On a snowmobile

3. In Chapter Five, the village pastor visits Grandfather. He wants Grandfather to do something. What is it?

A) Help repair his house

B) Look after his goats

C) Lend him a pipe

D) Send Heidi to school

4. In Chapter Six, Heidi arrives at her new home. Where is it?

A) Munich

B) Frankfurt

C) Zurich

D) Bad Ragaz

5. In Chapter Seven, Fräulein Rottenmeier receives a nasty shock at the dining table when she hears some unusual noises. What is the cause of these noises?

A) Cats meowing from Heidi's pockets

B) Dogs barking from Heidi's bag

C) A robin singing from under Heidi's straw hat

D) A goat bleating under the table

6. In Chapter Eight, music is coming from the schoolroom. Who is making the music?

A) Klara

B) Sebastian

C) A boy with a barrel organ
D) Dr Classen

7. In Chapter Ten, Grandmamma finds out that Heidi cannot do something and so decides to help. What is it that Heidi cannot do?
   A) Tie her shoelaces
   B) Tell the time
   C) Play the piano
   D) Read

8. In Chapter Fourteen, Heidi chooses to spend her money from Herr Sesemann on something. What is it?
   A) A new hat
   B) A wheel of cheese for Peter
   C) A white bread roll each day for Grandmother
   D) A book for Klara

ANSWERS

1—A
2—C
3—D
4—B
5—A
6—C
7—D
8—C

SCORES

1 to 3 correct: Perhaps, like Peter, you need to pay more attention at school! **4 to 6 correct:** A little help from Grandmamma and you will get top marks! **7 to 8 correct:** Not even Fräulein Rottenmeier could find fault with this score!

Glossary

alp	An area on a mountain where animals can graze
abscond	Leave swiftly
acceding	Agreeing to
ascent	Climb
askance	With a look of suspicion
assuaged	Eased
averse	Being against something
barrel organ	An instrument played by turning a handle
beseechingly	Pleadingly
blithely	With cheerful indifference
browbeaten	Intimidated into doing something
cantor	Someone who sings solo verses in church to which the congregation respond
cast aspersions	Spread doubt upon the integrity of something
conciliatory	Intending to make peace
contritely	With remorse
cowslip	A European plant with fragrant yellow flowers
cygnet	A young swan
deserted	Illegally left the armed forces
detriment	Harm, damage

dialect	A form of language specific to a particular region
dilapidated	In a damaged and run-down state
eaves	The part of the roof that meets or overhangs the walls
edifice	A building
elucidation	Explanation
emaciated	Starved
environs	Surrounding area
epileptic seizure	Convulsion or fit associated with epilepsy, a condition that affects the brain
equilibrium	Balance
felicity	Happiness
föhn	A warm southerly wind on the Alps
Frau	A form of address for a German-speaking woman
Fräulein	A form of address for an unmarried German-speaking woman, often a young lady
genially	With cheerfulness
gentian	A plant with purple or vivid blue flowers
haversack	A strong bag, often carried by walkers
Herr	A form of address for a German-speaking man
impairment	The condition of having a faculty or function that has been damaged
invariably	Always
livery	A special uniform

matins	A Christian service of morning prayer
mollifying	Appeasing anger
obstinate	Stubborn
organ-grinder	A street musician who plays a barrel organ
pallid	Pale
penitent	Feeling remorse
peremptorily	Insisting on immediate attention
pfennig	A unit of money in Germany, like an English penny, no longer used
prodigal	A person who leaves home or acts in a wasteful way, but then who returns home repentant or changes their ways for the better
proffering	Putting something forward for someone to accept
Red Indian	An old-fashioned term for a Native American that is now considered offensive
self-heal	A plant with purple flowers often used for medicinal purposes
spent grain	The malt that remains after the brewing process
St Vitus's dance	An old-fashioned name for an illness called Sydenham's chorea, associated with rheumatic fever
stem	To make headway against
surmised	Supposed without having proof of it
surreptitious	Secret
switch	A stick or shoot from a tree, formerly used as means with which to punish someone
tie beam	A horizontal beam, or piece of timber

trepidation	A feeling of fear and doubt
unerringly	Without fail
unremitting	Without pause
unwittingly	Unknowingly
unwonted	Unusual
vespers	A service of evening prayer
vigil	A period of keeping awake at a time when one is usually asleep

Treasure Island, by Robert Louis Stevenson
illustrated by David Mackintosh

The Castle of Inside Out, by David Henry Wilson
illustrated by Chris Riddell

Belle and Sébastien, by Cécile Aubry
illustrated by Helen Stephens

The Bears' Famous Invasion of Sicily, by Dino Buzzati
illustrated by the Author

The Wizard of Oz, by L. Frank Baum
illustrated by Ella Okstad

Lassie Come-Home, by Eric Knight
illustrated by Gary Blythe

The Adventures of Pipì the Pink Monkey, by Collodi
illustrated by Axel Scheffler

Just So Stories, by Rudyard Kipling
illustrated by the Author

The Jungle Books, by Rudyard Kipling
illustrated by Ian Beck

Five Children and It, by E. Nesbit
illustrated by Ella Okstad

How to Get Rid of a Vampire, J.M. Erre
illustrated by Clémence Lallemand

Anne of Green Gables, by L.M. Montgomery
illustrated by Susan Hellard

Pollyanna, by Eleanor H. Porter
illustrated by Kate Hindley

Little Women, by Louisa May Alcott
illustrated by Ella Bailey

Black Beauty, by Anna Sewell
illustrated by Paul Howard

Alistair Grim's Odditorium, by Gregory Funaro
illustrated by Chris Mould

Alistair Grim's Odd Aquaticum, by Gregory Funaro
illustrated by Adam Stower

The Secret Garden, by Frances Hodgson Burnett
illustrated by Peter Bailey

Alice's Adventures in Wonderland, by Lewis Carroll
illustrated by John Tenniel

Little Lord Fauntleroy, by Frances Hodgson Burnett
illustrated by Peter Bailey

The Railway Children, by E. Nesbit
illustrated by Peter Bailey

The Wind in the Willows, by Kenneth Grahame
illustrated by Tor Freeman

What Katy Did, by Susan Coolidge
illustrated by Susan Hellard

The Adventures of Sherlock Holmes, by Arthur Conan Doyle
illustrated by David Mackintosh

For our complete list, please visit:
www.almajunior.com